UNWRITTEN
CRIMES

KAYLA SERRANO

PAGE PUBLISHING, INC.
Conneaut Lake, PA

First originally published by Page Publishing 2021

ISBN 978-1-6624-3321-4 (pbk)
ISBN 978-1-6624-3322-1 (digital)

Printed in the United States of America

CHAPTER 1

I HIT A BRICK WALL. NOT IN THE LITERAL SENSE LUCKILY, BUT I DID HIT ONE WHEN it comes to my work. I shot out three best sellers, two of which are being turned into movies, and I was sure the third would be on its way eventually. My agent, Marcie, and publisher, Ben, recommended I take a break…a long-overdue break. My family always thought writing was easy; all you have to do is sit down and do it, right? Wrong. My best friend was my laptop, and I had not stopped in three years—no vacations, no parties, and numerous rough drafts. I was twenty-six and I was ready for retirement.

My tires turned onto the main road lined with trees. The sound of seagulls echoed, and the sun was setting. The old Mustang I've had since I was sixteen turned into the gravel-covered driveway. Rhode Island was my favorite, and the coast had always been inspiring. While I need a break, if my writer's block could disappear while I was here, I wouldn't be upset. I stepped out of my car to take in my surroundings. To say it was beautiful was an understatement. I was close enough to see the waves crash in, and the light breeze stole my hair from the sides and flicked them around my head. There were a few houses lined down the road, but it was quiet for the most part, which was exactly what I needed. The beach house was a baby blue with mint-green shutters; it was small from the outside, and I had only seen a few pictures of the inside, but I didn't need much, which was good considering I bought this place before doing a walk-through myself. What else would I spend money on? I threw my backpack over my shoulders and wheeled my two ginormous suitcases in. After all, I had no idea how long I planned on staying, and I guess if I really wanted to, I could move here.

The realtor said the key was left under the welcome mat, which seemed too obvious, but who was I to judge? It didn't seem like there was any crime here whatsoever, anyway. I unlocked the door and pushed my bags inside, locking the door behind me. The house was being sold with furniture, but I requested it be donated as I would want my own, so the house had nothing in it except a bed I had delivered earlier in the week. The closet in the hallway was a giant mirror. My blonde hair was a mess from the wind and from the eight-hour drive, I had bags under my eyes, and my shorts had a small coffee stain from hour three of my trip, but I figured I could shower and change after I get settled in. I rolled my bags down the short hallway and picked the bigger of the two rooms. The one I chose had a bigger closet and was facing the road as opposed to the ocean. After I put my clothes away and various other knickknacks, I jumped in the shower and felt like a whole new person. The bathroom had a claw-foot tub, which took up the majority of the space. Nola, the realtor, said it was one of the few things added to the place before it was sold. It didn't exactly fit with the rest of the house, but I felt lucky to have it already installed. I had some hair dye in my bag that I planned on doing before my trip but didn't have the time, so I quickly went from platinum blond to blond with blue ombre. For being here just two hours, I was starting to feel relaxed. I grabbed some pictures from my suitcase and found some nails and a hammer left behind in the utility closet. I hung up some pictures of my family and even ones of friends I had before I made it big. As I walked up and down the hallway, the wood floors creaked. I liked that. I admire a place with character and found this place to be beyond charming. The entries to each room were arched, every window had a lock, and the paint was in good condition.

I had zero interest in leaving the place even for food, so I ordered pizza, and there was a little shop down the way who delivered beer, which was absolutely amazing. It was nearly seven in the evening, so I sat out on the little patio looking over the ocean, drinking IPA and devouring a chicken and pineapple pizza. I knew the next day I would have to get furniture, which was not a problem since I had unlimited funds and appreciate a good deal. Most of the money I made from my first novel went to student loans and credit card bills; the rest of it went to family to help out, and that it did. In fact, they pushed me to take a vacation by myself. I would be a fool if I said I didn't move here partially because of my ex. We dated throughout college, and I was head over heels in love. He proposed to me in front of all my friends and family, and just as we started planning the wedding, I caught the bastard cheating. I have to say I am glad I caught him because I cannot imagine myself living my entire life with a liar. Unfortunately, I did not handle it well when it happened, which is what led me here. I found him cheating four months ago, so I set fire to his car. If I was an actor, it would have been plastered all over the news, but it actually was pretty hush-hush. I do not regret my actions by any means; it's not like I actually set him on fire but I went to therapy for a bit and realized I needed an escape, even if it was temporary. Matt was Satan's spawn without a doubt. I loved him or thought I did; now I realize it would have never worked, but I almost married him. I trusted the bastard, and it blew up in my face. I was all for a man, but I'd pass on commitment.

The peace was nice, but it was almost too quiet. The waves started to slow as the sun set, and then there was absolutely nothing. No light, no sound, no one. I thought about cracking the laptop open but decided to stay away for now. I'll get to it eventually. My cell phone buzzed, and my sister, Amberley, popped up on the screen. I hit Accept. "Hey, love!" I answered enthusiastically,

"Hey, sis, how was the drive? I'm assuming you made it okay?" Amber is two years older than me, but sometimes it seems like twenty. We started talking about guys when I was sixteen.

"It was a nice drive, and it's gorgeous here. It needs a little touch of home, but I'm glad I'm here. Maybe I'll never leave."

She laughed. "Great, maybe meet a man while you're there, okay? Mom wants grandkids, and I'm not breaking!"

I shook my head. "One day, okay?" which we both knew I only said to appease her considering I am swearing off marriage and kids until I can learn to trust again. We ended up talking for another hour before she went to bed. It was eleven at night, and the beach was eerie now. Fog rolled in and painted a dark, tormented picture for me. "Talk about inspiration." I shut the sliding door and locked it. I have an air mattress in the living room with my name on it. My editor asked why I didn't pick furniture out and have it sent so I could be comfortable right off the bat. I have money, but there are things I like to do myself, like handpick it all. Besides, I may meet some interesting townsfolk this way—I sure could use a friend or two. Hell, maybe my sister was right…a guy couldn't hurt as a plaything.

I killed it. I killed the air mattress with my pizza-stuffed body sometime in the middle of the night. Therefore my back was in immense pain, and getting up sounded like a nightmare. Throwing my hair into a bun, I grabbed shorts and a hoodie; there is no need to look good buying furniture. My old Mustang took me around town looking for some kind of store that wasn't surf-related. "Oh, come on, there has to be something!" I pulled into a parking lot in front of a general store, an old rickety sign dangled from the outside beams that read "Sandy's Cover General Store." It was quaint, and luckily, I hit a slow period. I opened the door, and a bell chimed. No one here, wow. I expected it to be slow, but no workers? "Somebody" by Smash Mouth played in the background as the fan in the corner mounted from the ceiling blew random strands of my hair loose. The door to the back stock area opened, and out walked a six-foot, light-brown-haired, scruffy, beach-sent god. The godlike body builder set two crates of soda down and shook his head to get a strand of hair out of his blue eyes—no, hazel. "Hey there, what can I do ya for?" His accent was definitely Southern, and that made him even hotter, which he needed no extra help with. I wonder what he was doing on the East Coast, but then again, people would ask the same about me. His jeans hugged his waist, and he had a light green T-shirt on, which did not hide his body.

"I, uh, well, I am actually looking for a furniture store, and I can't seem to find one around here."

He nodded and flashed a quick smile. "Ah yes, I thought you looked new."

He noticed, did he? "I'm assuming this town is so small you know just about everyone, huh?" I asked. I was hoping the answer was yes, maybe he could take me himself. To the furniture store, of course. Honestly, I always had dreams about moving to a small town where everyone knew each other. I love the close feel that was always faked in the suburbs.

"Basically! I'm Dakota by the way."

Wow, definitely not from here, but I'm okay with that. "Nice to meet you, Dakota, I'm Arielle. I just bought the small blue house on Seashell Lane." I beamed with pride.

His smile grew wider. "Very nice, what brought you here?" One eyebrow went up as in disbelief, and he must have seen my confused expression. "I mean...," he continued, "it's an amazing place, but not many people just move here."

I laughed. "I can't imagine why it's beautiful here, but ultimately I wanted a change of scenery. I'm taking a sabbatical from work." Okay, so I was not completely going into detail about what I do. I want to tell him what I do because I'm proud of it. I love writing, but I also have a lot of money, and I need people I can trust in my life. I definitely don't want this secluded and peaceful town to become a fan fest.

I told Dakota about what brought me to town, minus the money, of course. I left out some major details of mine, but I gave him the important parts. Dakota is a fascinating creature—turns out he not only ran the general store but also was a part-time fisherman down by the docks. His father is the preacher, and he had spent his whole life jumping from Rhode Island to Texas, which explained the accent. After about an hour of talking and multiple cream sodas, I was able to get directions to the nearest furniture store, which was about thirty minutes away into the next town.

I don't mind the drive, but at this point, I hated saying goodbye and I figured if I stayed another hour, I would be tearing off his clothes, and it may be a bit too soon for that. Quite frankly, it was nice to talk to someone who did not recognize my name. I went to back out of the parking spot, and I heard *clunk, clunk, clunk*. My car shuddered and turned off before I could move another step. Dakota came out, tilting his head as I stepped out of my Mustang and walked around the car. "I like the car, but I think you killed it." Dakota started laughing.

"Hey! Don't knock it. This baby has been with me for almost ten years and runs great! It's a classic!"

His hands went up as he continued to laugh. "We can get this fixed, no problem. Let's move the car to the side." I got back in the car and directed it while he pushed the car to the side of the building. I took a quick glance in the rearview mirror and saw his muscles showing off in the sun, glistening as if to torment me. I sighed and tried to refocus on the task, but the car came to a stop. Dakota came up to the window and bent down to face me, his hazel eyes flashing with charm, and I think I audibly gasped at the sight. He was something straight out of a Nicholas Sparks novel. "So I guess you'll be hanging out here for a while, huh?" He flashed a grin and winked at me. "I guess furniture will have to wait." Could I get a new car? Absolutely. Do I want to? No way. I have never been the flashy type. Besides I don't want anyone here questioning more about my life. Maybe I will run into someone who recognizes my name, but I'll deal with that when it comes. He opened the hood and tried to explain exactly what he saw, and the information flew so far over my head it could have been an airplane. I nodded and made sounds that indicated I was listening, but I was not.

"Arielle?"

I shook off the weird look on my face that slowly developed at some point during the under-the-hood tutorial. "I'm here, I was listening I swear. There is something broken, and it is bad." I smiled and flashed him my best attempt at puppy dog eyes.

He laughed. "Okay, note to self, not everyone is a car enthusiast." Two hours later, it was in working condition. While he was working, I bought some groceries for home and handed him what I owed. I figured since I took up hours of his time, it was the least I could do. Besides, I needed food. I'm not entirely sure what he did to the car, but it must have worked because my car was running without a problem. "Dakota, you are my new favorite person. I really appreciate everything you've done for me today." Was I flirting? Do I flirt? I set the groceries in the trunk and slammed it shut.

"It's the least I could do. You made today less boring for me. Online ordering steals my customers, so thank you for showing up when you did." He took a rag and wiped it across his head.

"I'll be around, and I promise I'll come to you for all my grocery needs and apparently car work. How much do you want to charge me for this, by the way?" I asked. I feel I should give him something for the extra work aside from buying groceries, which I needed anyway.

Without hesitation, he replied, "Dinner tomorrow night, I'll close early and pick you up at eight!"

I couldn't say no to that offer. We traded numbers, and despite my reluctance, I headed home.

CHAPTER 2

I TEXTED MY SISTER IMMEDIATELY WHEN I GOT HOME, AND NATURALLY, SHE CALLED me right away. "On a scale of boy next door to Mr. July, how hot are we talking?" was the first question out of her mouth.

"Both. I probably acted like a complete moron, but we are going out tomorrow night, so maybe he digs that?" I joked but honestly was still shocked he asked me out. I figured it would be more of a flirt-when-we-see-each-other thing. After my demonic ex-fiancé, I can honestly say I am not ready for a relationship. I am jaded with the idea of happily ever after, but I feel like Dakota can take my mind off that for a while. Amberley was begging to come visit after I described Dakota in all his glory, and the beach helped too. After I got off the phone with her and put the groceries away, I realized I still needed furniture. I drove the thirty minutes to the next town for a bed and bed frame, which worked out well because they had time for one more delivery later that afternoon. While they were working on other deliveries, I went to an antique store across the street and found an old kitchen set I would love to touch up. I've always had an obsession with shabby chic, and I could even make this my new hobby. This town was beautiful and serene. Jamestown looked exactly like all the postcards in Dakota's general store, but it seemed almost too quiet. Then again, I should not be surprised. The realtor told me the houses on either side of me are empty, and the season was slow. Perhaps that is what got me to sign the papers, and I truly felt as if I was being played at first, but

I am seeing it firsthand…the town is dead. Passing through town, there were little shops that lined the street, and flowers hung from every light post. It was getting later and later, but the sun simply faded into the background while pinks and reds flooded the sky. I passed by a small cafe with a giant wrought iron sign hanging from the side of the building. This cafe was nestled into the corner spot, and the outside was painted purple. Lilly's Kitchen looked like the perfect place to grab breakfast and get some brainstorming done for the next chapter of my series. *Trials of Courage* is meant to be a four-part novel series. Three of them were out, and two movies had been made. The third one should be announced any day now; I gave Marcie and Ben a free pass to contact me about it once they know the release date for the trailer. Parking my Mustang on the street, I walked up to Lilly's Kitchen to check out the hours. I peered in through the window; there were no more than ten tables with a breakfast bar filled with beach knickknacks. Cozy.

"Closed. Is anything in this town open later than four in the evening?" a masculine voice came from behind me. I caught a quick reflection in the window and turned around as the wind blew my hair back into my mouth. I choked on it a little, faltering. There stood a tall man in a sleek blue suit, tailored to fit him perfectly. It was obvious he was built underneath his white button-up shirt, and his shoes presented a near perfect reflection of me. He pushed his sunglasses to the top of his head. "I was hoping for a beer or a sandwich, but I might have to try to catch a hot dog cart down by the beach." He smirked and looked at his watch and back at me.

"Uh…are you talking to me?" I asked and glanced around. I am not used to strangers talking to me so casually, but I guess that's what I should expect here, although he did not look like he belonged here either. He laughed and looked around. "Yes, I am. Sorry if I startled you, this place seems like a Steven King novel at night. I'm Bryant, and you?"

His hand stretched out to meet mine. "Arielle. I just moved to town actually, so I am not familiar with the hours or atmosphere to be honest." I shook his hand and smiled. Not bad-looking. He had a five-o'clock shadow, and his blue eyes were so crystal clear that

I felt blinded. What is this place? It creates men that only dreams can draft up. I might never leave.

"Let me guess, honeymoon?"

I laughed. "Yeah, right. No, I am on sabbatical from work, and I am single." Wow, slick, you moron. I glanced down. "It's been a while since I've taken a break from work, and I needed a change of scenery," I explained to a perfect stranger. Something about this place makes me want to open up…might be the fresh air.

"I see, and what is your last name? I'm sorry, but you look familiar. What is it that you do?" he asked, head tilted and eyebrow up… When did that become sexy?

I choked a bit; he's jumping right to it then. "Taylor, Arielle Taylor. I don't think we have met, I would have remembered. It was nice meeting you though." I turned and walked back toward my car, leaving him standing there.

"Ms. Taylor?" Bryant yelled from thirty feet away.

I turned slightly. "Yes?"

He did a little jog up to me, which was funny since he was in a suit. "Look, I have been in and out of this town for a couple years now, and I'm bored here. I'd like to get to know you, if you don't mind?" He ran a hand through his hair, which was the only thing not put together on him. I considered it, I did, and I could almost feel my sister punching me in the face for what I was about to say, "It was wonderful meeting you, but I just moved here…temporarily, and I barely know you, so I'll have to decline. Have a great night!" I said with a quick wave and spun around on my heels and reached my door handle, while he stood there staring at me. I could have sworn the look was of disbelief, probably due to him never being turned down because he was handsome. I sighed. "Look, it's not you. I just…I ended things with my fiancé a few months ago, and I am not looking for anything right now, like legitimately, nothing. He cheated on me, and I figured it was happening, so I am fine, but it's still surreal because who does that? Who asks someone to marry them and then cheat?" I realized I opened my door and slammed it when his eyes widened. He leaned against the small sidewalk tree and smirked.

"Well, okay then. How about brunch? That's nothing after all. In fact, how about this? I will be here tomorrow for brunch around eleven in the morning, and if you'd like to join me, you can." With that, he walked away carelessly. I could practically feel the overconfidence radiating over him. I drove home trying to replay the conversation in my head. I acted freaking crazy, and he still wanted to see me—he must be insane. I was attracted to crazy people. Maybe Dakota was insane. I started to feel anxiety spark; what is making me feel this way? I was fine, everything was great, and all of a sudden, I was acting like a child with no control. I pulled up to a stop sign and dug through my purse. I know I brought my anti-anxiety medication. I felt the cap of the bottle at the bottom of my purse and lifted it up. A memory flashed quickly of me standing at a counter at the age of fourteen, waiting for my prescription to be filled. I glanced up to pop the pills in my mouth. In the rearview mirror, there were flashing lights, and suddenly my car was being pushed into the intersection full force. My head flung forward and hit the steering wheel, and my car skidded to a stop. "What the hell?" I reached up to touch my head. No blood but definitely a giant bump. I got out of my car slowly as the other car took off. My knees were wobbly, and my hands were shaking. My mind could not slow down. I was sitting at a stop sign. Where did the car go? A man and woman ran out from a corner building. I couldn't tell for what purpose, but they came up to me asking if I was okay and then nothing.

"Who does that? Who just hits someone and takes off?" a light feminine voice sounded.

"I don't effin' know! She got hit hard too, like *bam!*"

His hands must have smacked together pretty hard as it shook me fully awake. "Huh? What?" Everything was fuzzy, but the view was starting to shift into place. A short woman with platinum-blond hair weighing no more than one hundred pounds, decked head to toe in pastels, stood before me with a hot cup of something; next to her was a tall skinny guy with a man bun holding my keys. "Ooh, girl, you're awake. Good. Look, you were hit hard, you have all your limbs, and you *are* safe. My name is Brennan." He looked at me like I was about to cry. I nodded.

"Do you remember your name, baby doll?" the woman asked politely.

I barely heard her voice; she was so quiet, which I can't complain about now. "Arielle."

Brennan gasped. "Oh my god, like the mermaid?" His mouth dropped, and he started bouncing and stopped when he noticed I might vomit.

"Brennan, relax, you're going to make her sick." In response, Brennan rolled his eyes and took a step back. I tried to sit up and managed successfully without feeling like I was going to die.

The woman handed me a glass of water and what I hoped was aspirin. I took it graciously. "I'm sorry, I didn't catch your name?" I looked up at her, slowly bringing my feet off the couch to the floor to steady myself.

She nodded. "I'm Charmaine. We were on our fire escape and saw that awful car slam into you."

I looked around. "Where am I?"

Brennan crossed his legs and threw his hands in the air. He said, "Our kingdom, sugar," and winked at me. I sipped on some water as they retold the events and how they got me up to their apartment, which was on the second floor above one of the many surf shops in this town. After about an hour of Brennan talking about the surfers that always bring the smell of weed and sunscreen with them, I was ready to go. Charmaine walked me to my car, which they so kindly moved to the street. It had a huge dent on the trunk. "I love this car, it's a shame. You know, I think the hottie who owns the general store off Jenkins can fix this. I heard he is very handy." She looked at me with pity. "Are you going to be okay driving home?" she asked, not masking the worry.

"Thank you, Charmaine, I'll be okay. It was just a fender bender, I have a bump, but I'll be fine. I only live ten minutes away anyway." I opened the door slowly. "Hey, by any chance did you catch the license plates on that car?"

She shook her head slowly. "It happened so fast. I'm sorry, but I didn't see anything that could help." We said our goodbyes, and I thanked her again for helping me. The drive home was silent and mostly filled with me glancing in the rearview mirror every five seconds. The sun had set, and it was dark on the main road. Apparently this town was not a fan of streetlights by the beach. I walked up to my front door, and it was unlocked. I forgot to tell the delivery guys to lock it behind them. My bed was set up, so I grabbed an ice pack, some water, and my laptop. I ordered furniture to be delivered in the next few days. I gave up. I'm tired and needed rest. After I put in a few different orders for various side tables, couches, and chairs, clearing out the rest of Amazon, I started pacing slowly. I found myself taking a mini tour of the living room, kitchen, and bedroom over and over again. I was supposed to feel relaxed here, but in the last several hours. I met two men, had an anxiety attack, and was involved in a hit-and-run. This is insanity. I was not relaxed when I left the house, and I was expected to do it again tomorrow. "I must have broken a mirror recently because my luck is nonexistent." My phone buzzed a few times, letting me know I had a text message. I opened it to see an unknown number. *Hey, Arielle, it was wonderful meeting you today. I am looking forward to dinner tomorrow night.* It was signed the Car Whisperer, so I guessed it was Dakota. I had his number but had not saved it to my phone yet. Laughing at his text, I finished chugging my water bottle and went to text back, but I couldn't think of anything to say. What am I doing? I'm not ready for this shit. If I had to be honest, I was lonely, but at the same time, I need alone time. I came here to relax and write, not flirt and screw random guys. I'm not in college anymore.

I opened my manuscript to see the fourth installment of *Trials of Courage* practically bare. I feel like I cannot connect with my girl Paris anymore. I created her, but she was someone I once knew; she was becoming a stranger to me now. I figured it was a lack of development. She got too famous too soon, and she feels exposed. My e-mail dinged a few times as my inbox proved to be flooded with e-mails from Marcie and Ben. The only difference is

Marcie was shooting out statistics while Ben was asking how my trip was. I am unsure why he didn't just text me, but maybe he was keeping his distance. He and Marcie had a fling a while back. I don't think they know I know, and frankly I don't care. They both deserve to be happy, but it ended. I just don't know why. I quickly responded to their e-mails and got back to working on my novel, with very little success. I heard tapping on the roof and went out to admire the beach, assuming it might just be windy. The rain started pouring down, slamming down on the ground violently. I quickly closed the door and checked on each window to see if there was any water intrusion. The lights flickered; I looked up to glance at the fairly new light fixtures, and I could have sworn the realtor said they were one of the newer items in the house. I grabbed a beer from the fridge, wrapped one of the throw blankets I found the other day, and sat in the middle of the bare living room. The giant blinds covering the window in the room were raised up, and I watched the storm come in from the main road. The lights shut off, and I collapsed on the floor in exasperation. Are you kidding me with this? Gosh, it really takes me back.

"Mom, Mom! Mommy!" Running down the hall searching for my mom, I tripped over a toy I left lying there, or maybe it was my sister's. The lightning flashed through the windows, and thunder bellowed, shaking the house to its core. My mom was lying in bed, I tapped on her several times. My sister was in her room asleep, she slept through everything. I tapped my mom again on her face. "Can I sleep you with, please, Mom! I'm scared," I whined.

She shook her head, half asleep. "Ari, go to bed. Don't wake me up again."

I took a step back. "Mommy, please just this once?" She didn't respond. I turned around and knocked off a jewelry box on her night-stand. It was one of her favorites. It crashed to the ground and missed the carpet, hitting the hardwood floor, shattering into pieces. She jumped up quickly. "Arielle, what did I say! Look what you did!"

She went to grab my arm, and I took a step back, stepping on a broken piece of porcelain, cutting my foot. "Owww!" I yelled.

My screams didn't stop her from wailing on me. She slapped me, and I flew back to the floor. "If you would stop being such a baby and stayed in bed, this would have never happened! Do you like ruining everything I have? My life, my things! Get out of my sight!" I got up slowly and hobbled to the hall and fell. She slammed the door and ignored my cries. Amberley's door opened, and she walked out. Seeing the blood, she brought me to the bathroom and cleaned it out, bandaging it up. "Ari, you know better," she whispered. "Mom should never be woken up."

I sniffled. "Amby, why does she hate me? What did I do?" I tried to keep my crying to a minimum.

She shook her head and hugged me. "You can sleep with me tonight, and you really need to get over storms. They aren't that scary, okay? It's like…the angels are bawling, okay?" I nodded.

The storm would not subside. Dakota sent me a quick text, *Want to go surfing?*

I laughed, texting back, *You first, too busy playing outside with a metal rod.* I enjoyed this—storms are calming now, despite the miserable memories that come with them. I wrote my first novel during a ridiculous storm, and that set me up for life. I sat back down at my computer and started typing away as the wave of nostalgia flooded my mind. For about an hour I felt back in control of my life. My e-mail pinged, and I opened it immediately, expecting Marcie or Ben, but the e-mail address was unknown. *I love you. You waste so much time with losers, but I'll show you. You'll be mine and only mine. I will make you love me even if it is the last thing you'll do.* Wow, spam e-mails are getting intense. I saved it in my folder marked Funny, which is where I occasionally throw e-mails from the team or Amberley.

The next morning, I woke up to several packages on my front doorstep. Some of the furniture I ordered was next-day delivery, which was exciting. I spent all morning unpacking various items, which helped make it feel like home. I still needed to find something to wear to dinner with Dakota for tonight. I have next to nothing for this sort of activity, so panic started to spread. I have jeans and wedges, I suppose that could do, but then again I could almost hear my sister shaking me from several states over. There were a few shopping plazas in town I could check out; I suppose they were called boutiques, but I'll accept anywhere that has a nice dress. A wave of tension flooded my face; the events of the previous night attacked me, and I felt as if I was being slammed into them all over again. Taking it easy has never been a strength of mine, but I was determined to go out and live my life. I shuffled my feet to my closet where a few items hung. I threw my messy hair in a bun and pulled on some shorts and a tank top. It was summertime, and I'll be damned if I turn into a ghost.

After driving into town, I was able to find Leland's Fashion Boutique, a woman with grayish brown hair and blueish purple slippers in a rocking chair was sitting in front of it sunbathing. She looked so carefree and happy with her life. She opened her eyes, and her face lit up. "Oh hello, dear! Going inside?"

She continued to rock back and forth as I took one step and stopped, glancing up at the sign and back at her. "Absolutely, I have a hot date tonight, and I have nothing but torn jeans and flip flops with me."

She giggled at the image. "How exciting! I would go inside and help you myself, but it is too nice of a day to spend it indoors. My granddaughter is inside, and she will be glad to help you!" She closed her eyes and went back to sunbathing. I envy her but picked up pace and went inside. A small voice came out of nowhere: "Welcome to…oh! Arielle!" Charmaine popped up at the front desk and came around to give me a quick hug. Her blond hair looked brighter than it did last night, and her makeup was fully done. She actually looked like an entirely new person. "Hey, Charmaine, you work here?" I asked to verify I was not losing my mind.

She nodded enthusiastically. "My gran owns the place, but I run it. I'm sure you met her outside—that's all she does now, and I can't blame her!" She laughed. I explained to her my dilemma, and she grabbed me as forcefully as someone her size could and dragged me to one of the racks in the back. She started tossing dresses at me, and all I could see were colors—black, purple, blue, pink, red. "Uh, Charmaine, this is a first date, not a prom." I tried to sort through the dresses before I dropped each one on the ground. Charmaine grabbed them from me and hung them in the single dressing room they had. "Okay, welcome to your very own fashion show and tell! Put on a dress, show me, and then I'll tell you what I think!" She literally started jumping up and down clapping her hands, as if she has never shopped with another female before. Several dresses were tried on, some fit, some were hideous, and others made me feel like a disco ball. I shuffled out of the dressing room in a puffy red dress that made me look like a red swollen flamingo. "Do you have anything plain, short, and black?" I asked with hope in my eyes, the last bit of hope I think I could stretch for the day. Charmaine turned around and started rifling through the racks and grabbed a short dress covered in plastic. She removed the plastic and handed me the dress. "It is not black. but maybe this would work for you?" She smiled. The dress ended just above the knee with a sweetheart neckline at the top. The dress was not black, but it was teal with a black halter strap. It was stunning. I grabbed it and tried it on, expecting this perfect dress to not fit at all, but I was wrong. It fit flawlessly in all the right places. Dakota told me to dress up but would not tell me where we were going, so I was clueless and hoping this was not too much or even not enough.

I came out of the dressing room and spun around a few times. Charmaine was thrilled and beaming as if she were my fairy god-mother. It took her mere seconds to find shoes that went with it perfectly. "Charmaine, I really appreciate all your help once again," I said as she carefully put the dress and shoes in separate boxes.

She nodded. "Oh, it's my pleasure. How is your head by the way?" She tilted her head and examined me as if she had not been paying attention the last hour. I had a lingering headache, but nothing a few Advil could not fix, not that I told her that. "I'm fine, good as new!" I said my goodbyes to my fairy godmother and started to head home. I took a few steps outside when I nearly ran into a man talking to Charmaine's gran. "Whoop! My bad," I looked up as the man turned around.

He flashed a smile and took his sunglasses off. "Ah, Ms. Taylor, I was wondering if I was going to see you again." Bryant hovered over me as I took a step back. I swear this guy popped out of a magazine. Gran raised her eyebrows and went back to what she was doing. I can only assume this was her new routine. Bryant looked different today, less put together like our first run-in. He wore swimming trunks and a white undershirt. He sported Adidas slip-on shoes, and his hair was gelled up like a '90s boy band minus the frosted tips. "Bryant, we meet again. Are you following me?" I asked, raising an eyebrow, half joking and half wanting him to say yes. I feel like I was getting a lot of attention for no reason other than the fact that I was fresh meat to the area.

"You know, Gran," he started and shared a quick glance with the old lady on the porch, "Arielle here is the first woman to turn me down since I was in the second grade." Gran and I shook our heads as he nodded.

"Oh, is that right?" I baited him.

"Absolutely, and do you know what that does to an ego this big? Destruction. Pure destruction, and it is not safe for society. Truly, do you not care about the world you live in? Think about the children!" He dramatically threw a hand over his head and sighed. A good sense of humor was on his side, that is for sure. I laughed as he stared up at me as if I was a shiny object that he wanted. Desperation flashed in his eyes. I held the box the dress laid in and shifted it to my side, squinting at him—because I left my sunglasses in the car—trying to decide if it was worth it. Two guys? I did say none of it would be serious, so who cares, right? I stared walking to my car, feeling his eyes staring behind me. "Okay, okay, I surrender. I am busy tonight, but any other time this week works for me," I advised. He pumped his fist in the air, and Gran gave him a high five. "Perfect! I'll call you tomorrow with the details." He flashed a ginormous smile when he said that and winked before turning back the way he came. It wasn't until after he left that I realized I never gave him my phone number.

CHAPTER 3

THE HOUSE WAS FINALLY FULLY FURNISHED, AND IT WAS STARTING TO FEEL LIKE home, slowly but surely. As each moment passed, I found the concept of leaving here difficult, but no one ever said I was required to. Noon came too quickly, but the sun was out, and my fridge was fully stocked with beer. It was a gorgeous day, and it lifted my spirits even higher than I imagined. After all, this place was paradise. The beach was clean and quiet, the house next to me had people in and out of it. I was informed this morning that someone had rented it for the summer, meaning they won't be staying, so if there were any problems, I wouldn't have to deal with it long. Although I enjoyed the quiet, it was nice to see kids running around playing and actual individuals. I was starting to think I was the only person in this town that did not grow up here. Marcie started to lay off on the e-mails, which was appreciated. In theory, I have a lot more time to write this novel than we all originally anticipated. I appreciated her laying off; I think she is fantastic but somewhat overbearing at times. Ben, however, was e-mailing me every day, sometimes every other day if I was lucky. I wanted limited connection to the rest of the world right now. I chose to focus on the small bubble I have found here in Jamestown. The parents of the children came out to their back porch, which was lined with mine. The houses were maybe fifty feet apart. They waved and went about their business. I loved how easy it was. The waves broke up the sound of the kids screaming and the parents laughing. Although it was not a bad sound, I cannot lose focus of what I came here for, minus the guys. I suppose they were both serving as distractions and opportunities to get my groove back; it could be argued either way. I took a quick dive into the ocean for the first time; the water poured over me, and a sense of freedom passed through me. I was doing this on my own, away from everyone that had supported me and had demolished every bit of my soul. I had no good or bad influences within a five-hundred-mile radius and it felt fantastic. It had been years since I felt independent and strong. Being here was giving me myself back, and there was nothing I needed more than that.

After a lengthy shower, which mostly consisted of shaving my werewolf legs again, the window in the shower had a giant crack in it. I made a mental note to get it fixed. I stepped out, nearly slipping on the wet floor but steadied myself with the sink. Looking in the mirror, I realized I had a lot more work to do on myself before I felt comfortable with who I am. I tousled the towel in my hair a few times and let the wet blonde hair fall to my shoulders. The blue was still very strong, and this was the one night I wish it wasn't there. Before getting dressed, I dried my hair and curled it, threw some color on my nails, and did some deep breathing exercises. What if I overdress? What if I underdress? Is it too late to back out? When the hell was the last time I went on a first date? Finding the dress laid out on my bed where I left it, I dug through my closet to find shoes that would be appropriate. The anxiety was too much. Whipping out my phone, I decided to try to get some information from the man himself. He texted back almost immediately: *Dress casual, fancy gives me hives.* I laughed. Well, there goes the dress. I hung it up in my closet neatly away from my other things and set the heels underneath it. Digging through my dresser, I found a pair of jean shorts and paired it with a blue tank top and a plaid long sleeve. I slipped on a pair of matching blue Converse and left my hair curled and hanging down. By the time I finished getting ready, I still had a couple hours left. The nervousness was getting to me far more than I expected it to when I said yes to the date. My phone buzzed. Assuming it was Dakota or possibly my sister, I picked up the phone. Neither one of their names popped up; instead it was an unknown number. "This is Arielle," I answered, unsure if it was a telemarketer or not.

"Hello, beautiful. Thought I forgot about you?" the voice came through, sounding overconfident; I could almost hear the smirk.

"I was hoping you did actually," I said in return, hearing Bryant chuckle in the background.

"Okay, okay, I concede. You mentioned you were busy tonight. What time do you think you'll be done with your other date?" he asked in a serious tone.

Weird. "How did you know I had another date?" I glanced in the mirror with an eyebrow raised. "Also, where did you get my number? It's not even published," I advised.

"I had my bodyguard do some digging. He went through the police academy but dropped out for being too aggressive. I found it to be perfect."

I laughed. "Bodyguard? Are you a prince from another country and hiding it from me?" I shook my head and laced up my shoes, scoffing internally at the possibility.

"Hardly, but we can talk about that more tonight after your other date." He didn't sound mad, but it also did not seem to bother him at the same time—unusual.

"Seriously, how did you know? Did your bodyguard tell you or something?" I was dying to know, but I had a feeling he will not be telling me; then again it does not matter. I can date whoever I want, and I was not in a relationship with either one.

"Well," he started, "I was joking, but you confirmed it. Someone is paranoid!" He started laughing and let it die down as my cheeks flushed warm and red. I thought back to his original question; I have no idea what time my date with Dakota would be over, and I did not want to rush it. My phone buzzed again. It was Dakota: *Would you be up for meeting at six instead?* Wow, talk about perfect timing. I replied yes and started to consider my options. "Well, I am not entirely sure, but I might be free around ten or eleven," I offered up, not thinking about rushing from guy to guy. The thrill of it was overwhelming, but I felt invigorated.

"Fantastic, meet me at the docks at 11:00 p.m. and bring your appetite." He hung up the phone before anything else could be said. I glanced at the clock; it was barely four o clock. I had two hours to kill and refused to seem too eager for either date. My laptop was left open on my desk, so I clicked through a few playlists before I found the right combination of punk pop and eighties rock and roll. I danced around the room while also trying not to drench myself in sweat. I didn't realize I left the TV on until I saw the news headline flash on my screen: "Unknown female left for dead in motel." *Holy shit.* I turned off the music and turned up the television. "Witnesses say the woman entered the motel room, stumbling and loud. She was with a man who was regular build and wearing a black hoodie..." I turned the volume back down. Her body was found two hundred and fifty miles from here. She was my age.

I shook off the news report, ran into the kitchen, and took two shots to calm my nerves. It was nearly six o'clock; I had given Dakota my address earlier as he said he wanted to pick me up, which was cute. When I offered to meet him there, he refused; he really wanted to keep this a surprise. A Ford pickup truck pulled into my gravel driveway a few moments later. The butterflies in my stomach were erratic. I walked out and locked the door.

"Are you ready for some nostalgia?" he asked as I hopped in the truck and slung my seatbelt around me. His smile covered more than half his face, and his eyes reflected that too. His hair was just as perfect as it was when we met, and his facial hair was trimmed. Jeans hugged him tightly; even sitting down I could see that. He rocked a plain white T-shirt, and I realized the night could not get better than it was right now. "You look gorgeous," he said to me, eyeing me up and down like I was just seconds ago. I could feel my face turn red ever so slightly.

"Thank you. So where are we going?" Excitement crept into me. The fact that casual wear was the dress code threw me back into my comfort zone, despite the occasion. Dakota looked me in the eyes, which made it hard to listen to what he was saying. "The Ocean Breeze Festival is all weekend. It is full on candy, fair food, and those cheesy rides you see in every Romance movie. I love it, it's a blast." The smile that grew on his face told me there were positive memories, which I am grateful to be a part of now. I loved festivals growing up; no matter the season they were always a blast. My babysitter would always take me and my sister. My parents never did because spending time with us would be too exhausting, as my mother once said.

"I love fairs! Just so you know, I plan on eating all the fair food. You might have to roll me back to your truck." I rolled down the window, and the wind attempted to destroy my hair, but the hairspray kept it at bay a little.

Dakota hopped out of the truck and ran over to help me out. He grabbed me by the waist and slowly brought me back down the ground. "Are you ready to get your fair on?" He grabbed me by the hand, shut the door, and pulled me to the front of the fair entrance. It was like two kids in candy land. His hand was rough but also soft; he had working hands, which brought a bit of sexiness with it. The carnival lights flashed, kids ran around screaming with parents chasing them. A few balloons were rising to their inevitable home in the sky. The feeling of nostalgia, as Dakota predicted, was intense, but it was beautiful. After a bit of jogging, we stopped in front of the ring toss game. "Oh wow, I am terrible at these!" He handed me half of the bucket of rings and held the other half in his shirt.

"Everyone is! That's what makes it so much fun!" We both started tossing them, not hitting a single target as expected. People passing by stopped for a few seconds at a time to witness our failure and to laugh with us. Since the game was fairly slow, the game attendant gave us both fuzzy hats, which we wore with pride. We grabbed an elephant ear and fried ice cream, hopped on the merry-go-round, and chowed down. White powder got over my shirt, and ice cream fell on his. "We are a mess. Children eat neater than this," I said, laughing, nearly bent over in tears. His laugh joined mine as he slammed the ice cream into my face. I wiped the remaining ice cream off my face and back onto his. "Oh, the betrayal!" he yelled. Kids turned to look at us, and parents redirected their attention. This merry-go-round had terrifying horses that looked like products of nightmares, but it was still appealing. "This is a blast. Thank you for taking me here." I have not had this much fun in a long time; stepping out of my comfort zone was the best decision. He looked into my eyes, and I could tell what was coming. Am I ready for this? Is it going to be sloppy or sexy? I have never had a good first kiss; maybe they do not exist.

Oh god, please don't be awkward. He leaned in and stopped. I was not sure what came over me, but feeling his breath hit my face was almost too much to bear. I grabbed the back of his neck and brought him closer. I kissed him as hard as I could, and he returned it as generously and as passionately as possible. He wrapped his arm around my waist and pulled me closer. I refused to pull away; I physically could not. Eventually we both broke our connection; breathing heavily, I looked around and noticed the ride had stopped. Everyone who was on it with us had departed, and the entire line of soon-to-be riders was gawking at us. We both shared a glance and busted out laughing. He pulled my hand, and we hopped off the ride. He picked me up, spun me, and threw me over his shoulder. "Holy shit! What are we doing now?" I asked as he twirled me back to my feet.

"Anything you want, Arielle." His voice was husky and ragged; he looked me up and down, and I could tell what he wanted me to suggest. In that moment, I regretted making other plans tonight. His muscles were noticeable through his white T-shirt, and I could not help but stare. I must have done something right in a past life.

Two more hours passed of hopping on and off rides, downing as much fried food as humanly possible, and playing games that we could only lose at. The night went by far too quickly, and I had no interest in saying goodbye. It was for the best, though. I could easily see this interest in Dakota taking me farther, and the last thing I needed right now was more disappointment. The fair was right next to the beach, so the chill came over us quickly. It was slowly approaching nine thirty, and it was time for me to head back home. Dakota drove me back home safely, and we both refused to move any farther. Sitting in his truck, I felt like I was a teenager again. In my head I threw one leg over him and sat on him; he held onto my back with one hand and the back of my head in another. Again, this only happened in my head. Getting out of this car was going to be the hardest decision I would make in a long time. As ten o'clock quickly approached, I reluctantly slid over to my side of the truck, said my goodbyes, and headed for the door. My hair was less wavy, and I could feel a glow that I had not seen in months. "Arielle!" Dakota shouted from his truck.

I turned around to meet his eyes and smiled. "Can I see you again?" His eyes were pleading, and I could not say no—not that I wanted to. I winked. "Whenever you want, Dakota. Thank you for tonight. Text me when you have some free time. I'll be around." And I meant it. He backed out of the driveway as I opened my door. I could have sworn I locked it, but the door swung right open. I was not old enough to forget to lock my door. I took off my shoes and ran to my room. Bryant's driver was picking me up in an hour instead of having me meet him. From what I understood, that dress was about to come in handy. I fixed my hair to the best of my ability and freshened my makeup and breath. I cannot imagine how any date could get better than the one I just had with Dakota, but Bryant had something to him. Maybe he just caught my morbid curiosity. These two guys could not be any more different. I slipped the dress and the shoes on. I did a small twirl in front of the mirror and felt pretty for the first time in forever. Less than an hour later, there was a double knock on my door. I grabbed my black clutch and headed for the door. When I opened it, it was not Bryant but another man in a suit. "Arielle Taylor, Mr. Lawrence requests your presence at the docks." He guided me to the car, and in fifteen minutes, we were at the docks. I did not have the words to express the ridiculous size of the yacht that towered before me. There were hanging twinkle lights lining the entire boat and a singular table on the bow with two chairs. "Enjoy your evening, Ms. Taylor," the driver said and took several steps back, heading to the car.

Gorgeous did not begin to describe what I was seeing. It was pitch-black minus the twinkling lights, and all the windows on the boat were on, lighting up the scene entirely. If Bryant was going for romantic, he certainly hit the nail on the head. A few steps over there was a ramp leading to the bow. A small table stood before me with two candles and two wine glasses. The table was covered in a small white tablecloth, and the chairs held red bows around them. The ramp was taken by two men on the dock, and the gate on the boat shut. I turned around to see Bryant standing there in a suit. I was speechless. I spun around, slowly taking it all in as he came up to me and grabbed my hand, leading me to the table, letting me sit before pushing in the chair. "Bryant, this is incredible. You did this for me?" I sat in awe as he poured Merlot, which probably cost more than this boat, if I had to guess. I brought the wine glass to my lips, and I could feel him staring at me. I glanced at him with a goofy smile on my face.

He nodded and set his glass down. "I don't know how to do subtle, and I wanted to wow you. I think I succeeded." He winked. I could feel the heat start to rise in my cheeks, but I shook it off. I couldn't let this wining and dining tempt me into something more physical, at least not right now. The boat started to move away from the dock. "Whoa, are we really going out there?" My eyes widened, and he chuckled.

"Yes, not too far though. Just enough to look back at shore." He took another sip of his wine. "So, Arielle, how is your book coming along?" He leaned back in his chair. I could see a flash of smugness cross his face before it settled into a reserved stare. Did I tell him about my book?

I nodded. "Bryant, I don't believe we have discussed our professions. Are you a fan by chance?" I asked, part of me hoping he wasn't while the other part hoped he was. Nodding and shifting his weight forward, he pulled a book out from under his seat. It was the first installment of *Trials of Courage*. I wrote it several years ago on a whim, and it was what started my success. It was my story of luck. I only expected to self-publish and run my own bookstore.

I never imagined I would accidentally leave a USB copy of it at my favorite coffee shop and it would fall into the right hands.

He tapped the book with a pen, drawing me out of my flashback. "I actually am a fan. Believe it or not, I do read something other than business proposals." He poured another glass of wine for the both of us, and we clinked glasses. "I'm just surprised, that's all." He slid the pen over to me for me to sign the book. I signed it and closed the book just as our food came out, although I did not order a thing. It was my favorite—garlic chicken with roasted potatoes and asparagus. My mouth watered, and I did my best not to drool in front of Bryant. I looked up to him watching me intently. There was a twinkle in his eye I thought only existed in movies. "I hope this is still your favorite. I'm not going to lie, I found it on your social media page under a survey you did from four years ago." He laughed, shaking his head. "I am coming off as such a creep." For the first time, I saw genuine sincerity in his eyes. He was truly worried about being liked—either that or he was a very good actor.

I tried not to dive into my delicious plate immediately; eagerness is not always a positive trait on a date. "It may come off as creepy, but it is also a very sweet gesture. Hopefully you will feel comfortable not stalking me after tonight." I genuinely meant it because there was some charm to his actions but also slightly weird. Bryant was showing a side of himself that I did not expect. I looked out to the side of the boat. The water hit the boat gently. Because of how late it was, there was not a lot of action. We chowed down the food quickly but as polite as possible. I don't need anybody, let alone an attractive man, seeing me eat like a wild animal. While our food settled, we walked over to the balcony and watched the town pass us. The town was lit up almost as if it were just for us. I never received this level of romance from my ex, and we were together for several years. I just met this guy yesterday. As the town passed in front of us and the waves slowly wafted into the boat, we laughed and learned about each other. Bryant eased up on the businessman side, and I let my guard down like I did for Dakota. It only seemed fair. Turned out Bryant followed in his father's footsteps out of familial pressure, not because he wanted to. He gave me the spiel about wanting to make a difference, and while I am sure he meant it, it seemed too scripted for me. I kept finding myself judging him because he seemed too good to be true. Behind the womanizer, rich boy act, he was a sweetheart and a gentleman. I should have moved here years ago. Bryant had a beach house just up the road from me; his father sent him here to relax after he landed a huge contract, which he attempted to explain in more detail, but I was not one for business. Bryant knew who I was. Well, he knew what I did, and although I did not want anyone knowing and treating me differently, he understood a bit of where I was coming from, considering his background. It was nice to talk to someone who understood the importance of solitude and relaxation. The moon above us got brighter, and he moved his hand to my lower back. I felt tingles shift around my body. The captain alerted us that we were heading back to the dock, and the boat turned around. "Out of curiosity, is this boat yours?" I asked as he grabbed my hand and spun me away from the railing and pulled me closer. He snapped his fingers, and Ed Sheeran was echoing through the deck. His song "Perfect" was my favorite, and I swooned at the thought. He put a lot of care into this date and in such a short amount of time. It was crazy to believe how quickly my opinion about him changed.

"It is as of last week. My father never said when I had to come back to the office, and since we have a few partners who work overseas, it seems I can stay as long as I would like." He beamed with pride. It was clear he was desperate for a getaway from his regular, day-to-day life.

"It's beautiful." I admired it even more, trying not to look him directly in the eye because I knew what comes next.

"The boat is nothing compared to you, Arielle," he said as he leaned down to kiss me gently on the cheek. I was surprised, but I tried to not let the disappointment spread across my face. We swayed to the song as he dipped me. "Arielle, can I ask you an unorthodox and possibly intrusive question?" He cocked his head to the side as I came back up to meet him.

"Of course," I replied, and the song changed to another Sheeran hit that I couldn't think of.

"You make very good money from what I suspect of a writer of your stature. You have three novels and two films out. Yet you chose a small cottage in a random town in Rhode Island as your getaway. You drive an old beat-up Mustang, and you are by far the most relaxed person I have ever met. Why is that?"

Great question, and one I was not too surprised to get from him. He used his wealth openly and without regret. I was less open about my financial status. I thought for a minute because truly I had several reasons as to why I lived my life the way I did. "I grew up in a family that did not know how to manage money. Life was stressful every day, and it caused problems, but there were positives to it. My sister and I learned how to live on very little. We learned how to make a little go a long way, and as we grew up, we began to appreciate that more. Our parents were irresponsible, but we refused to be. I do have money, but I have shut out a lot of projects in a short span of time. After this novel, I am going to take a break for two years before I move on. I want to make sure I will be okay, just in case anything happens." We filled the next few minutes with idle chatter, laughing at each other's comments, and it felt natural. I could not be happier I did not have to go to a nine-to-five job tomorrow because by the time we hit the docks, it was almost one in the morning.

Bryant gave me another kiss on the cheek, which filled me to my core but also left me wanting more—fantastic tactic. We decided to see each other again, but I get to choose the place next time, which should be entertaining for me. I would love to see him in a normal setting and to see if he even knew what that looked like. Bryant stayed behind to ensure the crew had no troubles, and the driver took me home, although I do wish Bryant was the one to do it. I walked up to my front door for the second time in one night, a mixture of excitement and exhaustion settled in. Sound was pulsating through my front door. Odd. I unlocked it and took one step in. All the lights were on, the TV and radio were on with the volume on high, and every single window was open. I tore off running from room to room; everything mimicked the previously explored section. I was able to turn off the TV and radio just as a sheriff's car pulled into my driveway. "Oh, come on! Not tonight." I walked outside, and my neighbors came out almost at the same time. "Oh, miss, you are home!" the man said from his porch. He and his wife walked over in a hurried fashion. The cop's lights were going and reflected onto my face and the house.

"Yes, I apologize. I just got home to this mess," I said, waving at my house. "I have no idea what happened. Was it an electrical surge?" I glanced at the cop while my neighbors shook their heads.

"No, our house was fine. We questioned it at first, but when we looked outside to check on the other houses, it was only yours," she explained.

The cop was writing all this down before he even said a word. "Now I see here in the call to our station that there was a report of suspicious activity?"

My eyebrows raised. "I'm sorry, what?" I looked back and forth from the cop to my unnamed neighbors. The wife looked down and grabbed her husband's arm.

"Miss, we called the cops when we saw a figure run out of your house through the back door. I started screaming that I was calling the cops. It woke up all my kids. We came here for peace and quiet, not break-ins," he said as he embraced his wife. The cop stayed with us for another forty-five minutes before entering the house to examine it. There were no signs of forced entry. I told him I did not leave one window unlocked, but there was doubt in his eyes—doubt in me specifically. I thanked my neighbors Pam and Chuck for calling the cops when they did. Officer Clement inspected the house twice over and let me know everything was clear. After the excitement died down, the house was dead silent. My sanctuary became my hell, and I tried to push it out—"It was a one-time offense"—although deep down, I had my doubts, much like Officer Clement. I went through every window and door and locked it. I closed my curtains and blinds and left on every light. Tomorrow I am getting a home security system and new windows.

CHAPTER 4

"ALL RIGHTY, MISS, YOU SHOULD BE ALL SET. NOW LET ME WALK YOU THROUGH this." The older man from the security company finished installing the keypad and the door and window sensors. When I called this morning, they made an exception and came over immediately, making it here by nine in the morning. He wore jeans and a uniform shirt with the name Frank scrawled on the front. He installed sensors on every window and door sensors on the front and back. He walked me through the system until I felt comfortable with it. In turn, I gave him a beer and chocolate chip cookies...store-bought, of course. "Frank, thank you so much. I never thought I would need one of these."

He nodded. "It is just another added layer of protection. You live out here by yourself, and it is a nice place from what I can see, but you can never be too careful." And with that, he said his goodbyes and gave me his direct line in case I needed any help. I decided with all the excitement that today was going to be a stay-home-and-lounge kind of day. The first step was my medicine cabinet. It had been months since I needed my anxiety medication, and this finally was pushing me over the edge. The sound of my bare feet hitting the wood floors was soft, but it felt loud to me, as if I was suddenly hyper aware of my surroundings. Who tried to break into my place, and why? There was literally no crime rate in this neighborhood, and I had only been here a short amount of time. My anxiety made me irritable and quiet at the same time.

The best bet for me was to stay isolated so I could shrug it off. I opened the medicine cabinet in my bathroom and sorted through the various bottles until I found the prescription. "This is such bullshit." I twisted the cap and stopped. I tried to stare myself down in the mirror, but all I could see was fear. The memory of those e-mails from several days ago popped into my head. What if that wasn't just a crazy fan? The mirror reflected back despair and fear. This was not who I was anymore. Prior to moving here, my anxiety attacks would always be squashed by Ben. He was my rock, but he was not here now. In addition to despair and fear, guilt washed over me. I had not spoken to Ben in a while, at least nothing outside of work talk. Same goes for my sister. I guess there's nothing like a good break-in to make you question where your head is. I swallowed the pills and closed the cabinet. I just needed a quiet day of nothing to drown out the stress. I desperately wanted to open the windows to listen to the ocean waves crashing in, but I could not bear the thought of forgetting to close the window when I was done. I crawled into my giant queen-sized bed, wrapped a blue plush blanket around me, and turned the TV on to watch the trashiest show on cable. I needed something mind-numbing. I fell asleep watching some girl yell at her boyfriend and his brother claiming they were both the baby daddy.

My phone went off around two in the afternoon, which woke me up instantaneously, although I felt groggy and definitely had a headache. I answered the phone, "Hello?" without looking at the caller ID.

"Ari? Girl, are you good? I heard what happened!" A light voice came from the other end.

I pulled my head away to check. Yes, it was Charmaine. "I am freaked the fuck out, but other than that, I am great," I said, trying to sit up by pushing off my other hand. I had no interest in escaping the comfort. She started yelling in the background, probably at Brennan. I heard Brennan yell for me, something inaudible, really, but it made me chuckle, anyway.

"Look, you should not be alone right now."

I knew where this was going. "Charmaine, don't worry about it. I am not great company right now," I replied, rubbing my left temple.

I heard a few slams in the background and Brennan scream. "Ari, tomorrow, Brennan and I are coming over to see you, so you can do whatever you need to do today to heal, but tomorrow we are having fun!" she said with the most confidence I have heard from her to date. Brennan started screaming again, "Beach party, bitches!" I rolled my eyes; he was absolutely insane.

"I don't think a party is a good idea—"

Charmaine cut me off. "Actually, it is just what you need, a reminder that not all people suck." And with that, the conversation was over and I had no idea what I was in for.

I should probably open my e-mail to check on the status of things. I came here to get a distraction from my life, and now I need a distraction from my distraction... How crazy is that? I finally moved from bed and went to the back patio with my laptop and chamomile tea with an orange. My attempt at regaining some sense of normalcy would fail, but the effort was there on my part. Could the powers that be maybe give me a hand? Watching the waves come in slowly gave me no relief. The clouds rolled in, and the sun was nowhere to be seen. Of course, the day certainly reflected my mood. A car door slammed, and I jumped. Yeah, that'll show the car. I downed my chamomile tea and considered mixing rum in the next pot, sliding it over the table. I finally pulled up my e-mail. Marcie had held back on the e-mails entirely now, which was nice. My last call to her helped with that; I just had to inform her I was working on the novel and could not be disturbed. Ben, however, was quiet for a week because he was visiting family. I had one unread e-mail, which did not seem appealing because it was titled "My View." I might as well open it. How much worse could it get? There was no body to the e-mail, but there was an attachment. It loaded quickly, and my jaw dropped to the ground. "What the fucking hell?" I slammed my laptop shut and jumped away from the table, knocking my teacup over and shattering on the ground. The picture was taken outside my bedroom window this morning when I was on the phone with Charmaine. I was lying in bed with the phone in my hands. I thought the blinds were closed, but I was wrong. After having a panic attack, completely with my medication and two shots of tequila, I reopened my computer and forwarded it over to the sheriff, who called me immediately. "Ms. Taylor, I just received your e-mail. When was this sent to you?" he inquired.

I shook my head and tried to take another deep breath as I looked at the time stamp. "Maybe an hour ago. I was on the phone with a friend this morning, and that is what the photo was of. I had the security alarms installed, and I thought I closed my blinds." I was on the verge of tears.

"This is clearly someone trying to mess with you."

I rolled my eyes. "I have no idea who would do these things." I slammed my computer shut, hitting it one last time despite the possibility of breaking it. I heard the sheriff sighing on the other end; I could tell he was almost as frustrated as I was, but frankly, I cared less because I was the one being stalked. After getting off the phone with the sheriff, my phone started blowing up. I glanced at the screen, it was Dakota and Bryant. I almost felt dirty knowing the things I want to do to both of them, but I also felt guilty, almost as if they both knew I was talking to someone else. Well, Bryant knows.

Hey, Ari, I hope you had a good time last night. I can't wait to see you again—from Bryant. He even added an emoji smiley face, which did not surprise me. I opened Dakota's text message: *I think a beach day is needed once the sun is out. I'm extremely pasty, though, so make sure to bring sunglasses.* I laughed out loud. Dakota was the funny and gentle type, while Bryant had a kind side hidden behind his dark eyes. While Dakota had a structured life, it was filled with laughter—from what I understand anyway—and Bryant had a structured life in a different way; he was forced to grow up too quickly and thus acted out. They really were not too different. I can handle both of them; honestly it was hard to imagine doing two dates in one day again with everything going on. This was inspiring me to write, but I did not have a safe space to write anymore. Maybe that would change. I remembered what Charmaine said about having a party. I checked out the weather app on my phone, and it looked like it would be sunny the following day. I can beat this, I have been through shit, but I need to stay positive. After all, I have too much to focus on right now. A beach party was not a bad idea. It was Charmaine and Dakota's idea, so I felt like inviting Bryant was not a great route for now. Bryant knew about Dakota, but Dakota did not know about Bryant, and I was not entirely sure how he would take it. I mean, it was just one date. I texted Bryant first. *What are you doing tomorrow?* I wanted him to say he was busy or would take a rain check, but I could not guarantee that would be the case. *I am flying to Florida for a quick in-person meet and greet, but I will be back around ten at night. I can surprise you when I'm back?* I shot my fist in the air. "Score!"

Absolutely, but is it really a surprise if I know? Then I texted Dakota about the beach party for the next day, followed by Charmaine and Brennan, that the party was in motion. They were more than happy to bring everything needed, so all I had to do was be there. I could turn this into a positive, plus having people here might give me a sense of control. Last night, I completely understood why people fear silence, and I would rather not be put through that again. I felt a chill in my spine. The feeling of being watched rushed over me, and I ran to my room and called Amberley immediately. Telling my sister everything that was going on was not the smartest thing to do, but she would find it eventually, plus I needed someone I could talk to, and I missed my best friend. I needed to make it a point to call her more. After the first ring, she picked up. Sensing my nervousness, she started rambling, telling me to start talking, but once I heard her voice, all I could do was cry. Taking a deep breath, I told her about the friends I have made and went into detail about my dates, but none of that mattered at this point—not to her, anyway.

"Ari, are you insane? Come home now," she pleaded with me.

I shook my head and wiped tears away. "Not a chance. I like it here, minus the crazy stalker obviously. It was just starting to feel like home!" After an hour of going back and forth, it was decided she was coming to visit for two weeks. She called her boss immediately after getting off the phone with me to put the request in. My sister never takes time off, so I knew it was not going to be an issue. She worked at the local hospital as a nurse, which came in handy when I would try home improvement ideas from the Internet and they would fail…painfully.

After getting off the phone with Amberley, I was a bit calmer than before. I turned the knob on my stunning claw-foot bathtub that made me feel like I was a queen; the steam from the hot water quickly rose, covering the mirror. The bubbles were excessive, but I did not care. I felt like a kid in a candy store for the first time in forever, adding lavender bath salts to the mix. This was a little slice of heaven. Despite taking my medications, I poured myself a glass of Stella Rosa Red. I got my best ideas in the bath, so I brought my laptop in to dictate my words—best feature in my opinion. Slowly, the ideas formed for my novel even more clearly than before, using my current situation as my muse. Draping my legs over the side of the tub, holding the bottle of wine instead of the glass, I did not care what happened next. These stupid pranks I could get over, and I have Dakota and Bryant. Maybe I should utilize them more. I wonder what Dakota was doing right now, maybe working on another car or tidying up his store. An image of Dakota in his jeans with a white T-shirt flashed into my mind. That bright smile that could make your knees weak, and the scruff… it was not even fair that I met him in this time of my life. He was husband material, or at least secret lover material, or maybe that was Bryant. I don't know anymore. I flung my foot in the air, and the bubbles that latched on were free and flung to the wall next to the tub. I bet Brennan would flirt with both of them. Couldn't blame a guy for trying, of course, but I was glad to know they were mine for now. Charmaine would drool over them but would not dare try a thing. She did not seem like the type. More bubbles were flung at the wall, the bottle of wine was demolished, and getting out of the tub seemed impossible. My eyes fluttered shut.

A bottle of wine had never made me this tired before. I stretched out, and instead of hitting tub, I felt sheets beneath me.

"What the—that's weird." I moved around to make sure what I was feeling was real and sat up slowly. I wore my fuzzy lilac robe, and my hair was slightly damp. I glanced at the clock; it read 9:00 p.m. I got in the bath at seven; I don't remember getting out. That bottle of wine must have been strong, although I have had it before and never conked out like this. My head was fuzzy, and I felt dizzy when I sat up. Lying back down slowly, I noticed there was a bottle of water and aspirin on the bedside table. Reaching over and grabbing both, I realized I was paranoid. I must have gotten drunk and managed to successfully make it to my bed without chaos and destruction, which was a magical feat in itself. I got off my bed slowly and shuffled my way back to the bathroom to see what collateral damage I might have caused, but there was none. The bubbles were long gone, the bathroom was completely dry, and there were no signs I was even there. I thought I messed this room up in my drunken stupor, but oh well, it was about time luck was on my side. Turning off the light, I grabbed my phone and sober-texted Dakota, asking for him to come over. I waited twenty or so minutes and still no response—probably out on a date or working. Bryant was indisposed as well, and I was wide awake. I continued working on my novel and revising the parts I included before. Being hyperaware to my surroundings did not help my situation. I was a bit more relaxed now that I had some quiet time. Confidence was not my strongest suit; in fact, the lack of confidence I often have was a flaw, but I like to think I played it off well. I did a quick walk-through the house. All doors were locked and bolted, the windows were locked, and the alarm was set.

There was a knock on my door just after the alarm beeped, alerting me it was set. I walked over and peered through the peephole, but nothing was there. "All right, I am definitely losing it now." I rounded over to the couch to turn on the TV when another knock sounded. I turned the volume all the way down and stared at the door. I guess it could be the pipes instead. Another knock sounded. Through the front window, even with the blinds closed, I could see the sensor light go on, and then all I heard was incessant pounding. I dropped to my knees, hitting the hardwood floor. The sensor light went off, and I slowly stood back up. Debating with myself on if I should open the door or not, a rush of anger came over me—completely rational, of course, but it was begging me, if not forcing me, to open the door. I ran over to the door and threw it open. It was pitch-black, so I quickly turned on the porch light, and there was no one to be seen. I stood out on the porch looking around to see if anyone was hiding or running. Not that I would know what to do if I saw someone. Suddenly, I was face-first into the porch. "Fuck!" I turned around to look at my feet. I must have walked into something. The porch was naked aside from a giant can of what looked to be paint. I slowly got to my feet, readjusting my pajama pants. It was definitely a giant can of paint; red liquid was leaking out of it. Another sight of red caught my eye. It was my front door. It had a giant red X on the front of it. Awestruck, I stared at it far too long, wondering how I didn't notice that on my way out. Pushing the adrenaline rush aside, I ran inside to grab what I needed to clean up the mess. While doing so, I called the sheriff's station to report the vandalism. Feeling constricted, I collapsed to the ground in mental anguish. Why in the hell was this happening to me? I had not done anything wrong to anyone. Was this a crazy fan? I was sick of this shit. Rage began to build itself up again. I felt it bubbling at my core, but it only came out in tears. A cop showed up fifteen minutes later and helped me scrub the remainder of the paint off. The white door looked slightly tinted but nothing that couldn't be fixed. The cop sat out in his car the rest of the night so I could get some rest without worrying any further. I finished off another bottle of wine before bed, and I passed out without any regrets.

Another loud bang came from my door around 11:00 a.m. I jumped out of bed and grabbed the hammer from the toolbox in the utility closet by my room. My hair was everywhere, and the intimidation factor was only decreased by my mint green pajamas with llamas on them. "I am not dealing with this today!" I swung the door open and lurched forward with the hammer, and screaming ensued. Charmaine and Brennan took several leaps back, both screaming and holding on to each other as if they just emerged from a haunted house. "Arielle, what the hell, girl? Have you completely lost your marbles!" Brennan screamed as Charmaine grabbed the hammer.

They guided me back inside. "I honestly think so," I said and sat down on my giant recliner chair. My hair was a ruffled mess from tossing and turning, even after downing the bottle of wine I had barely helped me escape the events of the last few days. I told Charmaine and Brennan everything that happened. "Do you think it is someone you know?" Charmaine had one arm wrapped around me as Brennan shook his head.

"It must be a fan. Maybe this is like Misery." He had me at the Stephen King reference, and he wasn't too far off so far. Of course, I didn't expect to get taken and hidden away in a cabin. Charmaine ran into the kitchen to make several pots of coffee, and Brennan dragged me to the bathroom, locking me in so I could get ready for the day and look somewhat acceptable. I had no interest in showering, especially if we were spending all day in the sand. The sun was out, which was a nice change from the day prior. I cannot imagine getting through today without losing it. Holy shit, Dakota! At the first remembrance of my Southern gentlemen showing up, I perked up a bit. I glanced at my phone. I never got a text back from him from last night. That was a little weird, but I tried to shrug off my disappointment. Per Brennan's instructions, I got all dolled up and threw on a purple bikini. I hate being this exposed, but I would rather do what he says than hear him screech all day about how I could do better. He was like my mom but actually cared. When I got out of the bathroom, they clearly had unloaded their car with a keg and a tableful of snacks. Charmaine stood behind a table with various mixers and beer, finishing the setup. Both of my new friends were smiling ear to ear and were dancing to Top 40 hits. They seemed so carefree it was amazing how quickly they jumped into my life and integrated beautifully. Meeting them was a pro to moving here.

I slipped on a pair of jean shorts and grabbed several towels from the closet. Luckily I unnecessarily purchased oversized towels in every color even though in theory I only needed a handful. I threw them on the back of various chairs, which Brennan brought in from his Jeep Cherokee. Charmaine and Brennan invited a few of their coworkers. Heat spread across my skin the longer I stood outside. Brennan started the grill, while Charmaine grabbed a tanning spot on the beach, maybe twenty feet from where he stood. People I didn't know started to trickle in over the next hour. Drinks were being poured quickly, and it went from quiet and relaxed to crazy and loud. Music pumped through speakers that Brennan installed around the back patio. Even the neighbors came out with their kids and spent time in the sun. Luckily, the parents did not mind all the alcohol near the kids. Every time the sliding door opened or someone came around the house, I risked getting dizzy examining the area for Dakota, who still had not texted me back from the night prior. Charmaine bounded over to me as I stood with my feet in the water, holding a can of Bud Light. "No Prince Charming?" Her hair was up in a tight bun. She was decked out in jewelry with a bright gold bikini and yet radiated innocence despite looking like she stepped out of a 50 Cent music video. I shook my head and sighed. Attempting to hide my disappointment was impossible, and I know what was happening. I was getting attached. I literally met this guy a few days ago and went out with him once, but I wanted more desperately.

We heard a loud howl and turned around to see Brennan, finished with his setup and host duties, running toward the ocean with an inner tube duck around him just as he tripped over a sand mound and fell headfirst into the beach. Laughter filled the beach, but with every sound, I wondered, was it him? Was it her? Being surrounded by people felt great, but at the same time I don't really know any of them, and I like to think they would have no reason to hurt me. The more this thought marinated in my mind, the more I felt my airways constricting. Charmaine was typing on her phone and slipped it in the back of her suit. "Is this too much, or are you having fun?" Her eyebrow went up as if to say, "Don't lie to me."

A smile spread across my face as I pulled her in for a hug. "Thank you for everything. It helped, but I am just in my head right now." And I meant it. No matter what people do or say, I could not shake this awful feeling of helplessness. A low whistle echoed in my ear. Charmaine stared straight toward the house, and I turned around to see Dakota in swim trunks holding a bouquet of lilacs and roses. "Is that...him?" she asked, barely getting the words out.

"Yes...damn."

Brennan came back from the water. "Yeah, I don't care he's late. That man is fine." The three of us stood there staring until he approached me.

"I am so sorry I am late, Arielle. It has been a busy twenty-four hours, and my phone stopped working this morning, so I could not contact you." He glanced down at me, eyes sparkling with remorse, similar to a puppy who peed on the carpet. Yeah, I would have his kids.

I felt the same heat rising in me that I did when the sun hit my body. "It's totally fine. I'm glad you were able to make it." Charmaine and Brennan said their hellos and quickly left to play sand volleyball with my neighbors. Dakota grabbed my waist and pulled me to him. "I can't stop thinking about the other night," he said as he grabbed my face with his other hand and pulled me to him gently. His kiss was calming and steady, much different from the other night, and yet both left me dizzy.

"My life is crazy right now."

"Have you had a chance to explore some more?"

I slumped my head into his shoulder. "Barely, I have been so distracted with the break-in and the vandalism that I am not in the right headspace."

He picked me up and forced my legs to wrap around him. "I heard about that. These things don't happen here. My bet is on a fan."

He slowly walked toward the water. "I just find it hard to believe anyone is that hardcore crazy over an author. I got lucky I was in the right place at the right time."

His hands slid down my back, and a chill ran up my spine. "I'm sorry."

"For what? It's not your fault."

His face lit up, and he flashed a devilish grin. "Not for that, yes, but for this!" He threw me backward into the ocean. I made every attempt to dunk him, but he dodged every move I made. Laughing and swimming were not easy, but for a split moment, everything seemed normal.

The party started to die down, and people were trickling out slowly. It was a much-needed mental vacation from the insanity. Brennan and Charmaine cleaned up while somewhat drunk still, and Dakota called them an Uber. As I started picking up the remainder of the beer bottles, Dakota put away the speakers into a box, now named Brennan Forgot His Shit. We were both tired, and the day flew by so quickly that hardly a word was said. After packing up that one box, he came over to me, threw me over his shoulder, and brought me inside. As we passed the kitchen, my phone started buzzing, and Bryant's name popped up on the screen. I should answer that. I tried to get down, and with my attempt, Dakota countered it by laying me on the couch and kissing me intensely. I was addicted, melting, and completely in need of everything and anything he gave me. I could hear my phone buzzing over and over again. Bryant would have to wait; he would have his turn.

CHAPTER 5

INHALE, EXHALE, INHALE, EXHALE. MY YOGA MAT COVERED THE SPACE FROM THE back door to the beach entrance, and my phone pumped relaxing instrumentals through its speakers. The sun had barely risen when I walked out here with the hopes that it would relax me. Dakota spent the night last night, which was amazing, I could feel the extra energy coursing through me, but while it was positive energy, I still felt anxious. My legs were starting to shake, and my arms were sore. The alarm I typically have set started going off, playing AC/DC's "Back in Black." Standing up to stretch, I grabbed my phone, opened the sliding glass door, and tossed it on the counter. Grabbing two glasses from the cupboards, I poured orange juice in each one and brought them into the bedroom just as Dakota was sitting up, slightly disoriented.

"I apologize. I didn't mean to invite myself over just to get you into bed" was the first thing out of his mouth. It caught me by surprise, and then I laughed remembering that nothing actually happened.

Setting his orange juice down on the nightstand, I said, "No way. I appreciate you staying the night, and last night was fun. It was a nice distraction from the insanity that is my life lately." I took a large drink from mine and jumped back into the bed, sweaty and sore from my workout.

"Good." He pulled me into him. "Because I do not regret it one bit. I just never do these kinds of things." He still smelled like fresh sandalwood and mint. Why was it that men always smell like mint and something else? His hair was messy, but he was picture-perfect, anyway. We dived into deeper conversation of our lives. "I want to hear more about your novel." He looked me dead in the eye. My mouth opened to start explaining on impulse, but it shut immediately, locking the secrets away that I have been working hard to develop.

Smiling up at him, I patted his shoulder. "You'll just have to wait like everyone else. It's a surprise." I rolled out of bed to hop in the shower.

He feigned an offended look. "You don't trust me?" He threw a hand over his forehead and lay back. "Oh, how ever will I survive this heartbreak?" We both broke out laughing.

"Trust me, if I could tell you without my publicist wringing my neck, I would, but I cannot take any chances of a spoiler coming out, especially with the films being so successful." Pulling a towel out of the hall closet, I ran into the bathroom to clean up.

By the time I finished my shower, Dakota was up and dressed, trying to comb back his hair with his hand. "I think I can get a few chapters out of you!" he yelled down the hall. I wrapped myself my fluffy black towel and went to grab my phone from the counter in the kitchen. I had not even checked my texts or call log when I was on the patio. Desperation filled me to the point it was bubbling over. Yoga had helped other people, and I had the mat for months and never used it. It was not terrible exactly, but I probably would not do it again. Dakota was in the kitchen, elbows on the counter, staring at my phone. "Your phone was blowing up all night—someone named Bryant. Is that your publicist?" Blood rushed to my face. *What the fuck.* Trying not to run to my phone, I realized I never checked my messages when I brought it outside for yoga. He handed me the phone. "I did not mean to look, but it keeps going off. It might have been the sheriff."

I saw no jealousy in his eyes—not that he would be jealous, but he really considered Bryant to be a coworker of mine, which was adorable. Six missed texts and three missed calls. Wow...I never expected that from Bryant, but then again, he did say he had a surprise for me. Panic washed over me. What if he showed up here? There was no way, right? Dakota pulled his jeans up and threw his belt on.

"Don't let them ride you too hard. Seems a bit obsessive, but who am I to judge?" He gave me a kiss on the cheek and had to run to get the store up and running in time. Dakota only had two employees, and one was on vacation right now, so he was pulling extra shifts.

After watching Dakota pull out of my driveway, I dialed Bryant back immediately, hoping he was not too upset with the delay. The phone rang a few times and went to voice mail. He was probably sleeping. The rest of the morning was spent in front of my laptop and on the phone with Marcie.

"We miss you here in the office. You obviously don't stop by anymore, and Ben misses you clearly." There was no regret in her voice despite their prior relationship.

I glanced at my novel. "Marcie, I am not even halfway done, and this is supposed to be a vacation. I am far ahead of schedule. You have nothing to worry about, and as for Ben, I've been keeping him updated with my progress. He should be dating, not blowing up my phone." I laughed it off, but I was serious. I did not need another person up in my business all the time. As nice as Ben was, it was getting extremely annoying.

"Well then, why did you invite him to visit you?"

I paused. "What?"

Marcie chuckled. "Seriously, love, if he is driving you crazy, why did you invite him to your beach house last week?"

I pulled up all my e-mails and texts with Ben over the last two weeks. I didn't remember this, but I could have been so stressed that I did. But I could not find a single comment that could come close to an invite. "Marcie, I never invited Ben. You said he was coming here last week?" I asked, looking at my calendar. She must have misunderstood him; he would not turn up here uninvited. There was no way. "I guess I will call him back then, see what's up or something. That is so weird. I hope he's okay." My nerves were shot. Why would he come here uninvited? He really needed attention apparently.

The phone call with Marcie did not last much longer due to a knock at the door. I glanced through the peephole to see Amberley standing there impatiently with two bags. Amberley and I looked very similar, not to the point where people have mistaken us for twins, but from the back we were identical, especially when I did not have the blue in my hair. She is maybe half an inch taller than me but the same build. She was gorgeous, but I never felt the same. I threw the door open, and we slammed into each other with an overdramatic hug, causing us to sway widely, hitting the doorframe. She dragged her bags in and ran to the bathroom. A minute later, she emerged, jumping up and down while looking around.

"Girl, this place is gorgeous. It is so cute! I love it, wow!" Amberley walked around every room, not waiting for the tour. Sometimes letting her do her own thing was easier than forcing another way. As she dragged her bags to the guest room right across from my room, I opened a bottle of Moscato and grabbed two long-stemmed glasses. "How was your flight?"

She slid into one of the bar stools at the kitchen bar and shrugged. "Nothing worth talking about. It didn't crash, so that's a plus." She dragged her wine closer to her and attacked it with her mouth as I giggled. It was nice to have her here despite the circumstances. "You missed Dakota not long ago."

Her eyes bulged. "Damn it! Do you have a picture?" Her eyes pleaded as I shook my head. Condensation covered the glasses in thirty minutes, and they were refilled quickly. I started from the beginning on how I met Dakota and Bryant as well as the craziness that had been happening lately. She shook her head the entire time. "You should get a dog!" She slid across the hardwood floor in her socks and grabbed my laptop from the couch and began her search.

"A dog? Have you lost your mind?"

"You aren't twelve years old anymore. You can do whatever you want." She gestured to the house. "You are a successful writer with a beach house for God's sake. Get a Rottweiler or something." Mom never allowed pets when we were younger. They were no good, and if we brought anything home, she would get rid of it. In retrospect, I did not even want to think about the methods she might have used to do so. Mom never wanted to be judged, so she went out of her way to stay out of the judgment zone. I would not be surprised if she killed the animals with her bare hands.

"I guess a dog wouldn't hurt. I never considered it as a possibility." I rounded the kitchen bar and watched over her shoulder as she scrolled through various pet shelters in the area. Sadly, they were easier to find than furniture stores. There were so many dogs at the shelter it near broke my heart. How could you just choose one?

"You probably want a bully breed," my sister said without breaking contact from her research.

"I don't believe in bully breeds."

"Okay, well, neither do I, but it is easier than listing the big dogs that are on the list that will keep you safe."

"You know they aren't dinosaurs, right?"

She laughed, waving me off. After sorting through the various webpages, I grabbed her hand and my keys. There was no way a decision could be made online; I would need to see them in person. A guard dog was a great idea. I stopped midway and tossed her the keys. "I need to grab my meds. I'll be right there." Running down the hallway, I opened my medicine cabinet to grab my medication. It was not there. I slid into my room, which was diagonal from the bathroom, to check my bedside table and found them, popped one, and jogged back to the car. I could not forget to take these, or I would lose it at any second. We reached the first shelter on our list an hour before they stopped processing the adoption paperwork. Although reluctant, I hoped this would work out despite it being a last-minute thing. I could not believe I would be a dog owner by the end of the day. I had never taken care of a dog. What if I couldn't do this? Did they poop in sand? Walking up to the shelter, a woman was locking it from the outside.

"Excuse me, don't you close at four today?" my sister asked.

The woman turned around with a scowl on her face. "Usually, yes, but today is different. Come back tomorrow."

I took a step forward. "I apologize, but I was hoping to adopt a dog today, preferably a bigger breed that is protective?" Hope escaped my lips ever so slightly, and I felt a wave of nausea come over me.

She put her hands on her hips. "Look, dogs are not on this earth to serve you. If you want a slave or protector, get a man, not a dog." And with that, she walked away and did not look back. My sister and I stood there gawking at the storefront. Did that just happen? "Wow, she was pleasant," my sister said, and I stalked back to the car. "I thought you said people here were nice?" she asked.

"There is a bad seed in every group, I guess, not that she is wrong. Maybe this was a sign, I shouldn't impulse-adopt, anyway."

"Take me around town, then we can go to another location tomorrow or something." I drove her past Dakota's shop and the dress store where Charmaine worked. I wanted to introduce them, but the store was closed. Odd. When we got back to the house, I ordered pizza, and we broke out two more bottles of wine. *The Bachelorette* was on, and we lounged in our ridiculously embarrassing pajamas as Janna tried to pick her top twenty-five men. Amberley lay on the chair with her feet in the air, downing pizza and chugging wine like the lady she was, while I sat on the floor in front of the coffee table. My stomach had been bothering me with the stress and anxiety, but the meds were helping a bit. I glanced at my phone. Bryant still had not called or texted me back. As soon as I picked up my phone, a text came through, *What are you doing tomorrow?* as if Bryant could hear me. I wanted to hear about his trip. It sounded so flashy when he was telling me about it before, and he mentioned a surprise, which had me nervous but in a good way. I looked over as my sister reached for another slice. *My sister came to visit. She wants me to come home. I might be able to do something tomorrow night.* I set my phone down. I wonder if he was mad. He never answered my previous contact, and that seemed odd to me, but then again, I was not answering Ben in the same manner. "Would you be okay if I saw Bryant tomorrow or the next day?"

She threw her glass in the air. "Get it, girl! I'll relax on the beach, maybe get a fire going. You do you." Okay, she was drunk for sure, but I appreciated the support. Bryant wanted to see me tomorrow, but I figured one more day with my sister uninterrupted was a smarter choice, plus I hoped to get a dog tomorrow. We made plans for the following evening, and I felt good about that. I was excited to see him, but at the same time, I wished it was a few more days later. My gut was telling me I should have waited a bit longer before getting involved with two guys. Pulling my blond hair into a messy bun, I glanced down at my attire. If the guys showed up, I would be embarrassed as much as I hate to say it. I wore baggy blue sweatpants and a gray tank top. The bags under my eyes had been there a few days, and I had no idea how to demolish them. I was sinking into my couch, staring the TV down for hours. After catching up on older episodes of *The Bachelorette*, we went on an Amanda Bynes movie marathon, which was my favorite pastime. After several hours spent on the couch, we passed out completely wine-drunk.

I woke up to loud banging sounds. I glanced at the clock on the DVR; it read 3:15 a.m. Wiping the sleep from my eyes, I went to stand and nearly tipped over. My body was not ready to be awake. I grabbed for the nearest piece of furniture. Amberley must have turned the lights off at some point. I held on to the side of the couch as my eyes adjusted to the dark, and making my way to the door, I saw a figure through the side of the window. Peering through the peephole, I saw there were no one there. Weird. I opened the door an inch before it was slammed shut. "What the hell?" I turned around as Amberley held the door closed while locking it.

"Reset the alarm," she instructed, and I did so without further question. "Let me get this straight. You are being stalked and vandalized, so you open the damn door." I gawked at her, half asleep. "Seriously, you are not that dumb blonde in movies that gets sliced and diced first!" She ran to the back door to check it, and I checked every window as the adrenaline worked its way through my system. She peered through the front-room curtains. "Everything seems clear. We are so getting you a guard dog."

"Should we call the sheriff?"

"And tell him what? Someone was knocking on the door at three in the morning but we didn't see who?" She had a point. I took a few deep breaths and dropped my hands to my knees. This was exhausting.

"I am so glad you are here."

She leaned against the couch. "Dude, you need to move, whether it's back home or to another part of the beach. This is not okay. It's scary as hell." She turned on the living room light and sat cross-legged on the couch. The worry covering her face was enough to make it register in my mind; leaving was not something I wanted to do. I just wanted this mess to be over. Anxiety filled me again; the medication should still be working, but this was all too much. We both slept in my room, hiding under the blankets for added security as if we were young kids again hiding from the boogeyman.

The next morning came all too fast. It was definitely a good day to adopt a dog for multiple reasons. I wouldn't feel alone, and I might even feel protected at times. Amberley and I arrived to another shelter two miles in the opposite direction of the last. It was family-owned, which was a nice surprise. A little girl, maybe five or six, popped up next to us as her mother introduced herself and gave us a rundown of the shelter. "Here, grab my hand." She led me and Amberley to the back with her mother in tow. We went through the back swinging door, and there were several dogs playing in an open grassy area. It was clean, and the yard was also close to the beach, so seagulls were everywhere. There was one medium-sized black-and-gold dog in the corner barking at it, then it would stop and watch, and then it would continue to bark. If I had to guess, it looked like a Rottweiler. The little girl dropped my hand as we entered the room with the dogs, and she started running around playing with them. Her mother came up to us. "She calls them her brothers and sisters." We both laughed. What a wonderful world to live in. Everyone was good, and nothing could hurt you—to be a child again. Amberley went up to a Boston terrier, who was rolling on its back in the grass, but I had my eyes on the black-and-gold dog in the back. "Kira, her name is Kira. She has been here for six months and is our guardian angel." My eyes lit up. Besides being completely adorable, she looked intimidating at the same time. I whistled, and Kira's head perked up. She twisted around in seconds, staring at me and panting. "She might jump on you. She seems extra excited today!" the owner said.

Amberley looked up but was engrossed in the dogs jumping around her. I got down on my knees and prepared for the worst. "Kira! Come here, girl!" She took off toward me at full force, tongue hanging out, and slid right in front of me and sat down. Her back legs did a little dance, as if she was riddled with excitement. I smiled at her, and she jumped on me, licking my face. It wasn't until I tried to stand up that I noticed she was trying to sit on my lap. "How old is she?" She looked young but was strong.

"Kira is three years old but acts like a pup. She is loyal and spunky."

She was the one. "Let's get the paperwork!" Amberley did not want to leave, so while I filled out the paperwork, she stayed and played. Kira started following me around and licking my hand, which was adorable. Susan, the mother who was giving me the tour, provided a packet of information about Kira, including her most recent vet records. They provided a purple collar with her rabies tag and a black leash. Once her collar was in my hand, Kira started dancing again, making me laugh.

Hours later, Kira was adjusting to the beach house perfectly. On the way home, we stopped off at the pet store to get dog food, a few toys, and a memory foam bed. Honestly, she would probably stay in bed with me, but she would have options. Amberley was lying out on the beach. Not even ten minutes after getting home, Kira ran in and out of every room exploring while I set things around the house trying to make it feel like home. Dakota called me when I sent him and Bryant pictures of Kira. "I need her. Where did you get her?"

"Just down the road. It was a match at first sight, what can I say?" A stuffed lamb chop with a squeaker flew across my face, and she dove for it, sliding across the wood floors and into the kitchen. Bryant texted me the heart eye emoji several times and sent me pictures of him shirtless on the beach. Damn, good response. After two hours of running back and forth and throwing her toys for her to catch them midair, she passed out on the couch. A bit of drool hung from her mouth, so I took several pictures before letting her be. I dialed Ben's number to see what was going on with him; it went straight to voice mail. "What the hell, Ben, what is going on with you?" I asked my phone as if it were him. It was not like him to disappear, but then again he could have told Marcie one thing so she wouldn't bother him. I tried calling him again while glancing through the cabinets. Making food did not sound appealing tonight, but we just had pizza. Chinese! That was always a good option.

His phone went to voice mail again. The clock showed three in the afternoon, so I had a few hours to burn before I could gorge myself. Back to the laptop! Bryant continued sending me pictures that were not helpful in my desire to get any work done, while Dakota tried coming up with ideas for our next date. The store got busy, so his texts did not last, and Bryant went MIA. What was the point of dating two guys if they were busy at the same time? A few more chapters in and Kira was up and ready to go again. "Do you want a walk? A walk!" She started jumping and barking in excitement and ran to the door. As I was trying to meet her there, she would run to me and back again. I left Amberley on the beach; she was still tanning and drinking, living her best life, I suppose. Kira and I went walking down the small road to see what else was there without going into town. There were a few shortcuts through alleyways that were lined with flowers and vines; nearly every house was covered in them, and the roads were shaded over by huge trees that lined the path. Birds chirping distracted Kira from wanting to go straight. She kept glancing upward and barking at them, continuing her dance as she tried to move forward. The sun was not going down anytime soon, but the air was getting breezy. My hair whipped around my face. Leaves from the trees were spiraling up, and Kira tried catching them in her mouth unsuccessfully. After walking for nearly fifteen minutes, Kira dragged me over to an overlook where giant rocks lined the area and blocked any viewer from jumping into the water. Wave after wave hit the rocks and came splashing up. Kira stood on one of the medium-sized rocks and let the wind hit her face, ears flopping backward, and the same went for my hair.

I swung my drawstring bag from over my shoulder and pulled out a water bottle and a collapsible bowl for Kira. It was difficult to get her to turn away from the ocean, but she ended up drinking the entire thing. I sat on the rock next to her as she slumped over it. She looked uncomfortable, but she stayed there for twenty minutes while I popped potato chips in my mouth. "Wanna head back?" Her head perked up, and she tilted it, throwing her paw in my direction, which I took as a yes. Walking the same distance in reverse was exhausting. Just wanting to be home, I considered calling a car, but being a writer, I needed every step I could take.

Flashes of blue and red bombarded my view when I realized I was finally home. Two cop cars and an ambulance were taking over the entrances. Kira started barking and took off into the house, and I took off after her. "Amberley! Amberley!" A female officer blocked my way. "Move, bitch, this is my house!" I scrambled past her and into the front room. Amberley was being moved on a stretcher out the front door, unconscious. A cop came up to me, but I could not hear any words; the fear ringing in my head was too loud for anything else to push through. The lights from the cars and ambulance flashed through the windows and the opened door. Two cops stood in front of me as another one hopped in the back of the ambulance with Amberley. Almost immediately, the sound woke me from a daze. "What? What happened?" I stared out the door after my sister and then looked around the house. Everything was thrown about, the couch was pushed diagonally, the lamps were on the floor, and the TV was smashed. There was blood on the floor and partially on the wall. "Who…is that um… my sister's? Is she going to be okay? I need to go to the hospital!"

A headache hit me quick, and I felt a wave of nausea flow through me.

"Ma'am, let's step outside, please. We are going to get you taken care of." The young male officer put his hand on my shoulder and guided me outside.

The female whom I verbally attacked earlier spoke next. "Your sister is going to be okay—a few wounds but nothing the doctors at Memorial Health can't patch up. She is strong." Pictures were being taken of my new home, the home I thought would be a safe haven, but it had quickly become a danger zone. The ambulance was long gone, and I had no idea how to get to where she was. I was gone for an hour…just an hour. The officers took my statement after they told me my sister came in from the beach to face an intruder. They thought she tried to fight him instead of taking off, which sounded like her. Unfortunately, he won. Once she was done and heard the sirens, he took off. My neighbors once again were being nosy and intervened, thankfully. They deserved an award for best neighbors. The officers suggested Amberley might not have been as lucky if they didn't call when they did.

"The doors were locked, and so were the windows. The alarm was set!" In the beginning stages of my mental breakdown, the sheriff pulled up. I fell to my knees trying not to pull my hair out as the two officers went over the details with him. They walked away after a few minutes, and the sheriff knelt down beside me. "Ms. Taylor, we will find who did this."

My head shook back and forth uncontrollably. "No, you won't! I'm sorry, but you won't."

It was clear he was trying not to cry either, but it wasn't clear if it was out of frustration or remorse for not having found this guy. "We will get this place cleaned up as soon as possible. In the meantime, is there anyone you could stay with for the night?" He grabbed my arm and pulled me to my feet. The tears streaming down my face almost blinded me. Kira slowly walked over to me as if she was also feeling the pain, bent her head, and pushed it up against my leg.

"I don't know…maybe?" I knew a few people, I couldn't imagine piling in Charmaine and Brennan's small apartment with Kira now. The sheriff pulled away to communicate the next steps to the cleanup crew since the CSI just left. I picked up my phone, which felt heavier than ever. "Hey, beautiful," Bryant answered quickly. The sobs were overwhelming at this point, but I managed to get the story out with several breaks in between. "You're staying with me, I'll come get you right now."

"No, please. I need to go to the hospital and see my sister. I have no idea what is going on."

His hesitation was obvious, but he understood. "I'll meet you at the hospital then. Pack a bag, and Kira will not be a problem, I promise." With that I got off the phone, and the female officer who was calming me down earlier accompanied me inside to pack a bag. I grabbed stuff for Kira and myself for the night, and I packed a bigger bag for Amberley for the next few days. I ran into the bathroom and popped my anxiety pills and swallowed them dry, trying not to breathe too deeply and initiate another panic attack. As I grabbed a light sweater from the closet, the curtain covering my window was moving. Walking closer to it with the officer's eyes watching me, I pulled back the curtain. The window was wide open. "Seriously?" I took several steps back and ran into my bed. The female officer called for the sheriff to have CSI come back and examine for fingerprints along the windowsill. Twenty minutes later, my bags were packed, and I was out the door.

CHAPTER 6

Kira waited patiently in the car while I brought Amberley's bags to her. The doctors informed us she would need to be there for a few days to run tests and to make sure she was getting everything she needed. "I hate leaving you here, this is shit." As I leaned over the hospital bed with my hand over hers, her eyes were barely open. She was given blood, and stitches were on her head before I arrived and was about to go into surgery for larger lacerations or something the doctor said. I was still shaking from the entire experience my ears were hardly working.

Amberley was conscious, which was a plus. "I'll be fine. Please don't stay there tonight. I am begging you." Her eyes pleaded with me; the worry was not missed.

"I am staying with Bryant. Kira will be with me. The sheriff is having the cleaning crew go through the entire house to make it spotless. After that I am definitely selling it." I wiped a few tears off my face quickly, more so out of frustration than sadness. "Come see me tomorrow. As for now, let the doctors fix me. Then we will talk about it. I need some time to adjust. That was the scariest night I have had in a long time." My sister was strong, but even I could tell she was going to be having nightmares tonight. As two nurses came to wheel her into surgery, I returned my visitor's pass and jogged to the car. Kira was happily sitting in the passenger's seat watching the passersby. When she saw me, she started dancing and pouncing on the dashboard. "Hey, girl!" I slid into the driver's seat as a limo pulled up next to my car. "Yikes." Bryant stepped out with flowers and a half smirk, as if he had no idea what to do with his perfectly designed face. Kira jumped over to me and jumped up to him, licking his face with every jump.

"Bryant, I really appreciate this. Apparently it would take a while for the doors and windows to be fixed. Some of them were completely shattered." I swung two bags toward the limo, leaving my car at the hospital made me uneasy, but I was tired of driving. Bryant wore jeans and a light-blue sweater. His muscles were not very well hidden, and he was wearing reading glasses. He looked kind of like Clark Kent but blonde.

He shook his head; anger appeared on his face in a matter of seconds. "We will get this guy, angel, I promise."

As sweet as the comment was, I nearly scoffed. "Bryant, there isn't anything you can do. I doubt the cops will be able to figure it out either, otherwise they would have already."

Bryant put the bags in the limo and checked around my car before leaving. Kira hopped into the car and jumped on the seats before nestling down in the corner by the driver's partition. "Regardless, you will be safe with me. I promise." I smiled at him. While forced, I meant it, truly. We had not known each other long, but he was showing human decency that went beyond acquain-tances, and I appreciated that. The hospital was only fifteen min-utes from his house at the Point. The doctors said they would call me when Amberley was awake. I already told her the bill was on me or, at least, whatever her insurance didn't pay. I gave them extra to keep her in a private room, and the sheriff promised to have two cops outside of her door at all times. Broken, I felt like I was there.

"Once I can muster up enough strength to make it through this, something else happens." Bryant watched me intently. He squeezed my hand, lifting it up to kiss it gently. Tears welled up in my eyes, but I tucked them away so he couldn't see. The limo pulled up to a ginormous iron gate. The driver entered in a code, and the gates opened slowly. The limo slowly pushed through it. The mansion was a lot like the ones I would admire in old-school horror films. They were houses I swore I would never enter but would always appreciate from afar. "Don't let it intimidate you. There aren't as many ghosts as you would guess." I chuckled at his lame joke, but his face remained passive. "You have your own room, but it is close to mine. I want to make sure you aren't out of reach," he said with desire, assurance, or both. This was not the time to make a move, but I felt rescued, even though it wasn't necessary...or at least I wish it wasn't.

"I have never felt this helpless. I am no one special. Why is this happening to me?" I attempted to ask this sincerely and with a lot less pity, but it came out a bit whiney. He grabbed my bags despite the wide variety of staff he had here who was willing and paid to help. The mansion towered over us, built with gray and white stone. Vines stretched from top to bottom, but there was plenty of room for the glass-stained windows to shine through. Aside from the gravel driveway, which occupied a gorgeous angelic fountain in the middle, the remainder of the property was covered in pure green grass. One kind older man opened the door. Bryant caught it and urged me forward. The front room held an oversized chandelier, which shed light on the enormous handcrafted wooden staircase. Along the walls, which seemed to extend forever, were pictures of Bryant and his family; the occasional scenery photo held the rest together. "Incredible." I had money, but he really had it. I was living comfortably, maybe a bit more so, while he was living the lavish, rich life.

"Thought you might like it. Beth will show you to your room, and I'll come get you for dinner." He bent down to kiss my hand and walked down one of the many halls this place had, while a woman, presumably Beth, popped out of nowhere, nearly scaring the hell out of me.

Nearly jumping out of my skin got her attention. "Sorry, miss. I didn't mean to scare you." Her weak smile only proved she was trying not to laugh.

I returned her smile. "No worries. Um...where can I put my bags?" She snapped back to reality, mumbling her apologies, and took my bags from me. Kira, whom I forgot was with me, brushed up against my leg, forcing my hand on top of her head for a good scratch. "This place is ridiculous. How do you find your way around?" I couldn't look forward because the walls were lined with pictures, which covered a red wallpaper throughout the house. I imagined this place to be bright and cheery, but while it was stunning beyond belief, it had a darkness to it which I could appreciate. This was a place I would write in my novels.

"Oh, you get used to it, miss."

"Arielle. You can call me by my name, if you don't mind. Miss sounds odd to me," I said, giving her a smile, which she did not return.

After walking for what felt like hours, we arrived at a giant wooden door with carvings on it in the shape of vines. I was noticing a theme here. "Here we are, miss." Avoiding my gaze, she pushed open both doors, and I felt like Belle from *Beauty and the Beast*. The room held a king-size bed in a canopy, which was the center of several large windows, drawing in as much light as one room could hold and overlooking the beach. A giant wardrobe stood next to another door opening leading to a master bathroom. A couch was on the other side of the room next to a flat-screen TV. "If you need anything else, miss, ring the bell." The what? Before I could turn around to face her, the door clicked and she was gone. Behind the door was a small nook, which held a doorbell. That was unusual, but okay.

My bags were laid at the foot of the bed; my phone went off, making me jump again. "Hey, you." Dakota's voice was sweet and calming. The way he talked reminded me of simple summer nights; it was a nostalgia that never truly existed.

"Hiya, handsome, where have you been?" Exhaustion ran through me. I forgot what time it was. I was walking last night and everything was fine, and now the world was lopsided.

"I have been pulling shifts at the dock. Ari, I am so sorry. I heard about your sister. Is she okay?" When he said my nickname, it sent shivers down my spine—it reminded me of my childhood, and I was not sure if that was a good thing. Up until him, only Amberley called me that now.

"She will be. It's been a long day. I can't even get into it honestly. I am so drained right now." Dakota let me vent for a bit before I couldn't talk about it anymore.

"When can I see you? What are you doing tonight?"

Probably Bryant. "Nothing, just staying with a friend, Charmaine actually… I think I need to be here for now. How about I let you know. Hopefully soon!" I forced hope into my tone, maybe it was excitement. Regardless, it wasn't real. I wanted to see him, but what if he gets hurt next? I didn't even think about Bryant, but considering he has a fortress built around him, I would assume it was more difficult.

"All right, sounds good. I look forward to seeing you again." With that, he was gone. Hearing the desperation in his voice nearly killed me. I had not had this much positive and negative attention in such a short span of time, and it was messing with my emotions hardcore.

A three-hour nap was not on the agenda, but it actually helped a little. It was insane what a few weeks could change. I felt like a different person entirely. I was not the kind of woman who dated two guys or got stalked. I felt comfortable in unusual situations, and I feel uncomfortable in normal ones. I fell asleep on top of the blankets, waking up just in time to head to dinner. Fixing my hair as best as I could and wiping away the tears that joined me in my sleep, I opened the door to see Bryant standing there. "Holy hell!" I jumped back. "Am I going to need to put a bell on you! How long were you standing there?"

"I just walked up. Sorry to scare you. How was your nap?"

"My nap?"

"Yes, your sleeping time, slumber party of one?" His eyebrow went up in judgment, looking at me as if I had lost my mind.

"How did you know I took a nap?"

"Oh, I stopped by earlier and you didn't answer, so I just assumed especially with everything going on."

Of course, why did my mind go to dark places so quickly now? "Duh, well, I'm starved." He linked my arm in his.

"I was thinking we could eat on the patio overlooking the ocean. The waves have a calming effect."

"That sounds amazing, thank you! Also, thank you for letting me crash here during this insanity."

"Insanity?"

"Yes, that is what it is, to me at least."

"Well, to someone, what is happening isn't exactly insane. It's normal, it makes sense." The hallway only got longer from the last time I ventured through it. Door after door was passed, and they all looked identical. "Fascinating opinion. I guess I can't really care about someone else's feelings here, least of all the person doing this to me."

Bryant stared off. If I had to guess, he was choosing his next words carefully because in my mind he was almost siding with this lunatic. As if he read my mind, he said, "I get it, I just mean from a psychological standpoint, there might be something wrong with him." Kira was playing with one of the workers as he escorted me to the back patio, and to call it a patio was clearly doing it a disservice. "Anyway, how about we discus something more positive? How is the novel coming? I'm excited to read it." His smile was carefree; it was a look he seemed to be missing since he picked me up.

"It's not going as well as I had hoped, but I have a few different routes I could go. Honestly, I hate to say it, but everything that has happened is giving me inspiration. It is easier to imagine the horrors someone can face when they are happening to you." One step in front of the other and lifting my head seemed like a lot of work.

"Inspiration? Wow. That is a huge step from calling this guy a lunatic."

"Inspiration doesn't mean it's positive, it is simply giving me material to work with." The waves came in slowly. As we sat down, twinkling lights turned on, lighting up the entire patio. I would say it was romantic, but I feel stressed still.

"I'm not defending this guy, but it seems like, and maybe this is just me, it's a blessing in disguise."

"Are you fucking kidding me?" The cool breeze I was just enjoying wasn't enough. Feeling heat rise to my face, anxiety encompassed me, and the urge to deck him was the strongest it had ever been.

He grabbed my hand and squeezed it. "I am not saying you deserve this. I am just saying you could either let this destroy you or make you stronger." Mulling over his words which I probably have read on a fortune cookie before, I no longer wanted to argue, mainly because he was right. I had a brief moment of trying to be positive but let it go a week ago. I couldn't give up even though I was exhausted. "So please, tell me about your novel."

"Well, Steph is under control by the Agency as you know from the previous installment. Next, I want her to break away from the Agency with the help of James."

"James!"

"Yes, James! What's wrong with James?"

"He...wait, seriously? Look, James is an okay guy, but the fan favorite is Lucas." My eyes rolled to the back of my head and forward again. When the first novel came out, my growing fan base split themselves into a Team James and Team Lucas. There was a riot at a local movie theater which played on the news. It was hilarious but concerning at the same time.

"Okay, I'll consider it."

"There is nothing to consider. Lucas and Steph are team badass. Taking down the Agency is up to them, and James plays a minor role with no real talents. He's boring. Oh, but he's nice. Did I mention that?" A wild laugh escaped my lips. I've never had anyone tell me this before aside from various fan forums. "I have to say, I am extremely surprised you're that into my books. You seem like you live a busy life and have many people and companies relying on you."

"If I have to be honest, I listened to the audiobook. I would love to read the physical book or even the online version, but with how often I travel, it's easier to listen." His eyes dropped, and his interested smile mimicked them.

"Hey, that is nothing to be ashamed of. Physical book or not, those are still my words. It means a lot that you are a fan." A glass of wine materialized in front of me as a young man walked away quickly with an empty tray. I had not even noticed other people were here at this point.

My phone started buzzing in my pocket. I jumped up, fearing the worst. Bryant jumped back a bit in response. Dakota's name popped up, and relief washed over me. The doctors at the hospital stated no news is good news, so I did not want to hear from them. I hit Silent, promising mentally that I would call him later. Bryant tilted his head, and his left eyebrow shot up. I'll never understand how people do that, but it was attractive all the same. "Is that him?" he asked.

For a while, I forgot Bryant knew there was someone else. However, he had no idea what was going on with Dakota. "Is that who?"

"Come on, Arielle, is that the James to your Lucas?" He winked. Despite everything, he still held his self-confidence close.

"Sure, whatever you want to call it. Look, I am having fun with you, but I am not looking to get tied down to anyone right now."

His smirk said all I needed to know. If he wanted me, he could have me, *in due time*. My phone buzzed again. Assuming it was Dakota, I pulled it out to let him know I'd call him back, but it was the sheriff. "Hello." Bryant recognized the look I must have been making. He stood up and stared at me as if he was trying to hear the words through my eyes. "Ms. Taylor, I am sorry to bother you so soon after our last meeting, but there's something you should know."

"I'm listening."

"Charmaine Lockwood and Brennan Floot were found dead two hours ago in their apartment." The ringing of the wine glass I held reverberated in my ears as it shattered on the ground, the phone slipped from my hand, and I was falling into nothingness.

My eyelids fluttered. As I fully opened them, my head was pounding, and it was pitch-black outside. I looked up into Bryant's eyes as he stared down at me. My head was on his lap, and we were both in a bed—whose bed I honestly could not guess. "You fainted, I had a family friend—sorry, a doctor—check you out." He reached behind his back and ended me a bottle of water and two pills. "For your head, Arielle." I took the pills and sat up slowly, grabbing the back of my neck. The soreness was starting to spread. "You landed pretty hard." His eyes were filled with concern and pity.

"Charmaine…Brennan…" The words could not escape me. They were my friends. What reason did they have to die? I didn't need to know the details or, more specifically, who killed them. I knew who killed them—my stalker. Now who that was I still couldn't guess. Sitting by me, Kira was ready to lick my face and, with it, the pain.

"You're in your room. I brought you up here as soon as I could." Bryant edged off the bed and went into the bathroom. Water started to run and he popped back out as I chugged the bottle of water on the nightstand. "Okay, I really don't know how any of this works, but you need a break. The bath is running, and I loaded it up with a shit ton of bubbles."

"You didn't need to do that. It's very sweet of you though." I slowly slid off the bed, feeling as if every muscle in my body was aching. I should have asked questions to the sheriff like why or how. The why wasn't as important in theory. Unfortunately, there wasn't always a motive, and the whole fainting part didn't exactly help.

"There is a glass of wine and the remainder of the bottle by the tub. I'm going to give you some time. I'll be two doors down if you need anything." I nodded slowly and trudged over to the bathroom. My clothes were off in seconds, and then I eased myself into the tub. The hot water rose slowly. I felt like I was hit by a train, but I also felt like a princess. Times were getting weird, I guess. My head tilted back as I let the wine rush down me, and exhaustion creeped back. As my eyes were closing, something small and black caught my attention on the ceiling. "What the fuck?"

When I woke up, the bubbles had evaporated and the wine bottle was tilted over. A drop served as proof it was all gone. As I drained the tub, I felt my numb legs, making it difficult to stand up. I pushed off the edge of the tub and tried to slide over the side, knocking my thigh into the giant stones surrounding it. That will be a nice bruise. Glancing in the mirror, my hair was all wet, and my makeup was running still. I looked like a hungover mess, but…turning back to look at the wine bottle, I only had a few sips. The bottle was light, but it was definitely empty. I was certain Bryant said he had just opened it. Head pounding, I bounded to my bed where Kira was snoring away. I should check to see if any messages were left from the hospital or Dakota. Walking over to the side table, there was nothing there. I picked up my bag and searched it. No phone, and patting down the bed proved to be unhelpful. I could video chat it from my computer, and the alert would guide me to it. Where did I put my laptop? The same search fiasco occurred with the laptop to no avail. I could feel my face getting hotter.

"What the fuck?" Little black thing. Ceiling. I ran to the bathroom. Glancing up in the corner, there was nothing there—must have been a spider or something. I splashed cold water on my face and took a deep breath. I was on edge, but where the hell were my things? I threw my hair in a wet bun and grabbed a pair of sweatpants and a tank top. Kira had stirred a bit, but she was not getting up anytime soon. Bryant said he was three, no, two doors down from me. Opening my door, I noticed the hallway was quiet and barely lit. Instead of the regular beach-house blue, this place was mansion red, which came with some spooky decor. The giant wooden doors were lining the hallway, and I counted two down, then slowly opened the door to not scare him.

"Look, I know what I'm doing, okay? You have nothing to worry about. This isn't my first time." Bryant's voice was hushed but frustrated. "Yes, I know. That was not supposed to happen this soon. I know…I know…I've got her wrapped around my fin- ger, okay? Whatever…I've got to go." He gently placed the phone down, and I took a few steps back. Bryant? Bryant was doing this? Why? I had to get out of the place. Did he drug me in the bathroom? I sprinted back to my room and threw everything in my bag. Oh shit…my phone and laptop. I quickly surveyed the entire room again. I'll have to leave without them. "Kira, let's go!" Her head perked up, and she jumped off the bed. "Shhh!" Her ears went down, but I could sense the determination in her eyes. I opened the door slowly. No one was there. I took a few steps out with Kira at my side.

"Arielle, you're awake." Bryant was behind me. I turned around with a smile on my face. "Yes, I feel much better too. I don't want to take any more of your space and time, so I think I will visit Amberley and see the progress on my home." I could feel sweat at the top of my head. His eyes showed pity, but that was all it was, a show. "Ari, your sister is in the hospital, and two of your friends were murdered. You should not be alone right now." He took a step forward, and instinctively I took one back. His eyebrow shot up as he looked me up and down. "I know this is not a good time to ask, but are you okay?"

"Yes, I'm fine, considering. I just feel like I need to be alone right now."

"You said you were going to visit your sister."

"Well, that is different, she's family." A silent moment passed between us. Kira took a step in front of me. Good girl. "Look, I appreciate it, I do. I just have to go like now."

"Arielle, you are not safe out there. I can keep you safe."

"No, I have to go." I booked it, running down the hallway and down the stairs, trying not to fall with Kira at my side. I kept turning back to see if anyone was following me, but there was no one. Pushing through the doors without resistance, I was outside. The gate was open despite the time, and we kept running. Kira had no issue with it, but my asthma was starting to act up. Halfway down the road, I collapsed onto a small grass patch near a Stop sign and called a cab.

CHAPTER 7

"HE HAS GIVEN US NO PROBLEM IN THE PAST. HE HAS LIVED HERE HIS WHOLE LIFE, Ms. Taylor." The sheriff leaned over in his chair, sweat dripping down his forehead and exhaustion in his eyes.

"I know how this sounds, but I heard that phone call—"

His hand went up to stop me. "Do you have concrete proof?" His eyes never moved to mine; he kept looking down.

"Sheriff, he was talking about—"

Hand still up, he questioned more sternly, "Concrete proof?"

"No."

"Then we have nothing to discuss. You are free to return home." I had no interest in going home, but the nurse called me to advise Amberley made it out of surgery and was sleeping soundly, which was comforting. The deputy brought me and Kira home. She jumped out of the back of the squad car and ran to the front door, doing her dance as if nothing was wrong, and for a split second it made me smile. Turning the key took forever, as if time slowed down and the world put itself on mute. Once the door opened, the deputy drove away, and the world made sound again. The oceans waves were the loudest, and second place went to the kids next door running around and screaming. Kira ran to the couch and jumped on it, rolling around it like everything was normal, and everything seemed normal, except for the fact this place was covered in my sister's blood twenty-four hours ago.

Behind me, I locked the door and set the alarm. Sitting on the couch with Kira, I took a deep breath. I could only handle so much of this and, the police were nowhere close to figuring it out. I knew they wouldn't take my concerns seriously when it came to Bryant. I needed one quiet night, was that too much to ask? *Ding-dong.* Fuck this. Throwing my legs off the side of the couch, I quickly went to open the door, expecting it to be a cop, but it wasn't.

"Ben?"

"Hey, miss me?" Ben stood tall, with shaggy brown hair, crisp green eyes, and glasses. He was definitely nerdy cute but not take-me-home cute.

"What? How? Come in!" Several emotions hit me at once. Ben was still physically here and alive. "Marcie has been worried sick about you! What the hell, man?" He brought his two bags in and slid them by the door.

"I know, I have gotten every single message she has left, but I was on an adventure and did not want to answer to my ex-girl-friend. I am sure you could understand." That I did. If my ex contacted me today, I would not respond, even if I worked with him or not.

"Well, I did miss you, and I am glad you're okay. You had us all worried sick." I gave Ben the rundown of everything happening, implying that was the reason I had not answered him. I told him what happened to Amberley and that she would be back soon and then explained what happened to Charmaine and Brennan and that they definitely would not be back.

"I haven't been hiding, but I have been exploring. Why was everyone so concerned?" he asked, confusion washing over his face.

"Marcie said you were coming here nearly two weeks ago," I spewed. I was legitimately concerned about this, and it was the last thing I needed on my mind.

His mouth formed an O shape. "Ah yes, I told her that so she would not freak out. You know how that goes." I could see it—my concerns floated away, at least for that subject.

"You can grab the couch because Amberley is staying in the guest bedroom."

"You know you could afford a bigger house."

"I know, but I like how quaint this place is. Well, I did anyway. I might move."

"Don't let this get you down. If you like this place, then get it, but trust the cops on this one. They are the experts." He had a calming way with words—maybe that was how he got to be great editor.

"Why don't you get comfortable? I don't plan on going anywhere tonight, so maybe we could just hang out and go over what I have so far?" I was hoping he would say yes. I have been struggling hard with this novel, and I was sure half of it was exhaustion and the other half being stalked. "Good news. Amberley is being discharged from the hospital this afternoon. The sheriff is bringing her right here." I poured a glass of wine for me and grabbed a beer for Ben. He sat in front of his laptop editing one of the many novels he signed up to do. He could work on multiple novels at a time without getting confused on the plots; it was impressive to say the least.

"Hell yeah, that's great! Did she mention if she was going home soon?"

"No, she still wants to hang out here for a while. She's scared, but I think it is more for me than for her."

Ben shook his head to acknowledge he understood. "She's strong. If something like that happened to me, I would be on the first plane out of here."

"We are stubborn women, if you hadn't noticed." I laughed.

"Agh!" Ben grabbed his arm, his face clenched, and he took a deep breath.

"Are you okay?" I poured some of Kira's food into her bowl before she got cranky. The metal on her collar clinked against the bowl.

Ben got up, holding his arm. "I'm fine, just a little sore. It's probably cramped up from driving long distances without breaks." He rubbed it generously before settling back into his spot on the couch. *Ding-dong.* I forgot I had a doorbell. Racing to the door out of habit and sliding across the floor, I almost forgot being happy was a dangerous thing to be. Ben chuckled as I opened the door.

"Dakota!" Before I could consider control my body, my legs propelled me forward and my arms flew in the air, wrapping around his neck.

"I'm sorry if this sounds creepy, but I have missed you, and it's only been a few days, but I couldn't wait any longer." Those words were all I needed to break down. Dakota grabbed me, and we moved forward into the house.

"Uh, hi?" Ben's voice went up an octave. Okay, this might get awkward.

"Hey, man, I'm Dakota." Dakota stretched his hand out.

Ben watched him for a second before extending his hand. "Ben, nice to meet you," he replied and shook his hand.

It went silent for an eternity before Dakota cleared his throat. "So, uh, how do you two know each other?"

"Coworkers," I said.

"Friends," Ben quickly said over me. I looked at Ben as if to say shut up. Whether he saw it or not could be debated.

"All righty, Dakota and I are going to go out for a bit. Help yourself to the fridge and any places that deliver. You'll probably find a menu in the kitchen." Nodding at Dakota back the way he came, I grabbed my purse from the hall table, quickly closing the door behind us.

"Where have you been?" Dakota turned to me, seriousness in his eyes. "You weren't at home or the hospital. I heard about your friends. I was scared shitless!" His voice raised with each word.

"Look, I'm sorry, things have been a bit crazy for me lately. I was staying with a friend."

"Who?" The question made me take a step back, not just because he was asking but because he felt he had the right to ask.

"My friend Bryant."

Dakota stared at me like I slapped him in the face. "Okay...so by friend you mean...someone else you are seeing."

"I mean, kind of. It's not a big deal, okay?"

"Good, then stop seeing him"

"What? You can't ask me to do that."

"Sure I can. You have to choose. You can't string both of us along."

"Dakota, this doesn't sound like you. I like hanging out with you, but this isn't anything serious. You know about my recent breakup."

He shook his head, covering it with his hand, and started laughing. "You've been stringing me along since we met. I've been there for you or at least tried. The least you could have done was tell me the truth!"

The door opened, and Ben stood there. "Is everything okay?" he asked, glaring Dakota down like he was ready to punch him. It would have been an unfair fight—Dakota was at least four inches taller with more muscles, but I applaud Ben's willingness.

Dakota backed up a few feet before turning completely around, heading to his car. "When you decide, let me know." Leaving it at that, he drove away. I stood on the front porch in shock. What the hell just happened? "Two guys, Arielle? For real?" Ben stalked inside and busted open another beer. The tears formed in my eyes but never released. Judgment on top of all this? Where was the slack or pity? I would legitimately take that over any of this bullshit right now. I slammed the door, causing the pictures on the walls to shake, and stormed off to my room like a child. I popped my anxiety pills and chased them with a can of soda I had in my room. In a matter of seconds, my body slammed to the floor.

I woke up on the floor with a throbbing headache. Unsure how much time had passed. Glancing around slowly, everything else seemed fine. I sat up, feeling the weight of my body alone. I wanted to throw up. "This has got to stop happening." I pushed off the floor with one hand and grabbed the bed with the other. I felt like death, and my legs nearly gave out, but I braced myself, leaning into the bed. Glancing on the floor, I could see red smudges. My hands were covered in paint—no, blood. I burst into the hallway, flicking on the light so I could see there was something sprawled on the wall. I took a few steps while holding onto the wall. I fell on the ground in seeing the wall covered in blood. There were a few handprints on the wall that must have matched mine if I had to guess. "What, what the? Oh shit. Ben! Ben!" I screamed at the top of my lungs, looking back and forth frantically. "Ben! Holy shit!" I forced myself back up and ran to the bathroom. The mirror had writing on it: "Call the cops and die." Ben was nowhere to be found in the apartment. I checked myself repeatedly for any open wounds. The blood was not mine; it must be Ben's. Why was it on my hands? I opened my pill bottle and sniffed it; there was an acidic smell to it. The pills were covered in some kind of liquid. Tossing it out, I started wiping down the mirror and pulled out all the cleaning supplies in the house to clean off the blood from the hall. Tears streamed down my face; I was alone, confused, and covered in blood. I finally made it to the living room, where it was spotless. I turned around to examine the hallway again; there was no blood. Bringing my hands to my face, I saw they were flawless. The sliding glass door opened and shut.

Ben walked in with a beer to see me standing in the hallway half naked with my hair looking like a lion's mane. "Hey, you're awake." He casually walked over to the breakfast bar and sat down, taking a sip of his coffee. "Are you okay? You look a little crazed."

Standing there, staring at him and back at the hallway, I might be a little crazy. "Ben…how long was I out?"

He glanced at the clock for a second or two. "Maybe two or three hours?"

"I think I need to see a doctor…" I turned around and walked slowly down the hall until I made it to my room, sitting on the bed in complete silence. I went back to the bathroom five minutes later and dug my pill bottle out of the trash; it still smelled acidic. "At least I am not completely crazy," I whispered to myself. I put it back in the trash and covered it with toilet paper. Sitting in silence, I tried to remember everything that happened up until this moment; things were fuzzy, and I felt like I was blocked.

My phone went off—a text from Amberley. *Hey, sis, I won't be coming over. I am heading back home. I'm sorry I just don't feel safe.* I guess I should not be surprised. I called her, and the phone went to voice mail. I thought about calling my mother for a split second, wondering if they had been in contact, but the thought quickly escaped me. Panic filled me. An overwhelming sense of urgency to cleanse this entire house swept through me and left as quickly as I could remember. I was losing my shit. I could hear Ben moving about for a few minutes before pure silence. I thought about going out to talk to him, but remembering our last conversation before my black out, I decided against it. I was still pissed off. How am I expected to churn out a novel, let alone live in this place any longer? I need to get out. I dialed the number to my realtor to tell her this place needed to go up for sale immediately. "I'll rent it out if I have to."

"Well, Ms. Taylor, in all honesty, you might have to because it is a buyer's market right now, and we have heard of what has been going on. It will be a challenge to sell it now."

I slowly and quietly beat my fist against my head. "Of course I understand, we can take that route. Can you find me something else? Anything else?" I gave her a price to work with, and she said she was on it. I told her I did not care where it was or what it looked like, I just needed an out.

The next morning, I slowly got in the shower. Every muscle in my body felt achy, almost as if I was beaten up on a regular basis and hit by a semitruck, followed by a bunch of smaller trucks that held spikes. Okay, I was getting out of control. Regardless, I felt like shit. The steam rose fast as the water hit my body, practically searing it off. I needed to be scrubbed of this entire trip. This entire place was a disaster; it was my own personal hell for whatever reason I still could not figure out. I kept pushing the curtain back a little to check the bathroom entirely; suspicion and paranoia had settled in, at least this I could recognize. I watched the water hit me and run down to the base of the tub. I would cry if I had the energy, but I was too weak. I will survive this, I hope. Charmaine was dead, Brennan was dead, my sister had been scared off. The tears nearly came out at that thought. I came here to be alone, or at least I thought I did. I actually came out here for a new start, and I couldn't have that. On the other hand, whoever was doing this was trying to get to me and break me down. Even if I have to fake it, I needed to try to not let this get to me. I needed to be strong. I just didn't know how to anymore. I shampooed my hair three times before deciding to get out of the hot shower. I could do this. My senses were clear, and my hair was clean. I could do anything…for now.

The sun was beating down, and the ocean looked gorgeous. The sand was a light beige, and it reminded me of the Bahamas, which sounded pretty nice right about now. I grabbed my laptop and three bottles of water to prepare for my day on the patio. I needed to get something done on this novel, especially since Ben was here watching my every move. "Need help editing?"

"Not until I am done!" I sprayed some water in his direction. "I actually have inspiration. Unfortunately, it came at a price." I tried not to think about Charmaine and Brennan; they just met me and were wonderful people, completely undeserving of what they got.

"Well, you're going to write an amazing novel, once I get through fixing it!" He laughed, and I flipped him off.

"How long are you staying again?" I half-joked, half legitimately curious as to when he was leaving. I liked having him here for the sole purpose that there was someone to talk to, even though he kept staring at me like I was a prize to be won.

"You are an amazing writer, Arielle. The best writers find inspiration in the oddest form and strangest places. It is okay to explore the darkest part of your mind. It will only make you better." With that, he ran out to the beach, diving into the water and shaking it off like dog that just got a bath.

I received a ping on my computer from Marcie: *Is Ben coming back? I don't want to come and get you both, I hate working from the office alone.* I didn't know what to say, I wanted to invite her here to bridge the awkward gap between me and Ben, but either it would get worse because she was here or someone else would die. I was not entirely numb to the entire experience, but I had a feeling the killing won't stop. *I wouldn't suggest it, things are not safe here.* The dots showed she was typing, but after a good ten minutes, nothing was sent, indicating she was angry, but I was going to let it go. A few hundred words later, I found it harder and harder to concentrate. Ben left the water and came trudging over to me, the sand getting stuck in his toes causing him to slow down. "So I was thinking…maybe we could do dinner tonight."

I kept typing. "Yeah, sure, whatcha thinking? Pizza or Chinese?"

He was staring at me, starting to laugh. "I was thinking like actually going out to dinner, like a date or something." He ran his towel through his hair and shook it like a wet dog.

"What if we just had dinner as friends?" I tried not to look at him or laugh. Uncomfortable situations made me act even more awkward, and I knew it wouldn't be well received by him.

Marcie pinged back. *We need a few chapters of your novel, otherwise they may pull the deal.*

I scoffed. "Marcie is out of control. She said the publishers will pull the deal if I don't send a few chapters."

Ben, clearly hurt but jumping into work mode, raised an eyebrow. "Yeah, right, your novels are only making them millions a year, and you split the film right. She's blowing smoke up your ass. Ignore her." And with that, he went inside. A wave of relief passed me when he left. I felt his disappointment radiating off him, and I had no doubt he would have stayed there and stared for as long as he could.

Halfway done with my novel, I shut my laptop with ease. The waves were the only thing making noise in a five-mile radius. They were almost able to calm me down but not completely. What was next? If I had a psycho fan following me around, hurting the people I care about, then when did it stop? With me? If I thought about this like I would a novel, they would go after the weaker targets first, and then it would escalate. At some point, there had to be a big finale, so what was that? If I could figure out that finale, then I could make it out of this alive. Being negative didn't sit right with me, but the sheriff's department was not helping at all. A sense of freedom was all I wanted when I came here. I felt like I was being backed into a corner and could not escape, and now, I had no one who would stand by me. I needed to find a sense of normalcy. Ben opened the door, and Kira ran out, nearly tackling me in the chair I was sitting in. "Hey, baby girl!" I rubbed my hands on her, and her back end went wild. He stood there at the door watching me for another minute before slowly shutting the door. Okay, this was getting awkward fast. At this point I would rather be here with only Kira and risked getting killed then have him here with me. Kira noticed a few seagulls landing on the beach and took off. I followed her as fast as I could without tripping on mounds of sand. She didn't go far without me, which was an unexpected plus—no training needed. The sun was going down, and the sky filled with pinks and oranges of every shade. It was beautiful. Kira chased seagulls back and forth until they learned landing by a giant dog was not the smartest move. She happily trotted over to me with pride for her seagull-scaring accomplishment and sat down in the sand. It wasn't until I was convinced staying on the beach wouldn't solve all my problems that we got back up and went inside. Ben had moved his things into the guest bedroom this morning, possibly meaning he was not heading home anytime soon. Unsure of how to ask him to leave, I said the only thing I knew could point him in that direction. "Oh hey, I was thinking it would be nice to have Marcie here so we can get some more details about what they intend for the book release."

Ben glanced up at me with a look of shock. "For real?"

"Yeah, might as well get it over. I invited her, and I am waiting to hear the details now. Better now than later. Besides, I am almost done." I whipped out my phone, pretending to check something when really I was drafting a text to Marcie to invite her here. Marcie had her awful moments, but if I wanted Ben out, she would need to bring those moments here.

CHAPTER 8

Two DAYS HAD PASSED, AND I NEEDED TO GET OUT OF THE HOUSE. I HATED IT AT home, but things were starting to die down. I still could not escape the feeling of being trapped. Marcie would be arriving today, and Ben was picking her up from the airport. A light breeze whipped its way through my hair, twirling it around an invisible finger. The sun was out, but it wasn't hot, just comfortable. I left everything technology related at home, but I had my Taser the sheriff gave me, which left me barely at ease. Catalonia's Coffee had their doors open, with smaller tables set outside the store front. I walked in and ordered peppermint hot chocolate, despite it not being winter. It always calmed me down. Bringing my hot chocolate outside to feel the breeze again. For the first time in weeks, a sense of calm rushed over me. Shouting and bangs—that was what reached my ears before anything else. I looked around to find the cause of the disturbance. Three stores down on the other side of the road, a guy had been pushed over a set of tables and chairs into the road. A car passing on the street swerved out of the way. Another guy ran out of the store and tackled him. It was Dakota. The guy in the middle of the road was Bryant. I grabbed my drink quickly and ran across the street. "Seriously what now?" By the time I reached the storefront, there was a small crowd of people watching.

Dakota threw another swing at Bryant, but Bryant blocked it by elbowing him in the gut and then tackled him to the ground. Dakota was able to get out from under Bryant and pushed him several feet back. "Stay out of the way, Feld, this doesn't concern you!"

Bryant spit blood out of his mouth. "Kota, this is stupid. Knock it off, man!" Feld? Kota? Do they know each other?

Dakota started laughing. "Seriously? You always get in the way, every single time." Dakota threw another punch, but Bryant dodged it. They exchanged punches and kicks for another two minutes until the cops showed up. The cops, who were much smaller in size compared to both Bryant and Dakota, barely pulled them away from each other. Dakota had blood dripping down his face, and Bryant's eyes were swollen. Both were hauled off in different cars.

"That was the most action this town has seen in years," an old woman whispered to her husband. Parents who had their kids with them rushed them back to the cars so they could get home, probably dreading the millions of questions they would receive. I stood there dumbfounded. As both Dakota and Bryant got into their respective cars, they saw me. I saw remorse and rage in both their eyes, which left me confused. The cars drove off to the station. Should I meet them there or leave them? It would probably make things worse if I bailed them both out. Not that either one of them really needed the help, but it doesn't take a genius to know that was about me.

I drove to the station against my better judgment. "Ms. Taylor, I am afraid to ask." The sheriff saw me, and his face went from smiling and happy to grim in seconds.

"No worries, Sheriff, I am just here to visit the MMA fighters you brought in recently." He let out a light chuckle, one I did not think he was capable of. I was almost offended by his initial reaction to me, but I know it was not personal, even though it felt like it. Dakota and Bryant were put in cells facing each other. An officer escorted me to the back to see how they were doing. When I stopped in front of both of their cells, no one said a word. The officer gave me a chair as requested, and I sat down between them. I pulled out my laptop and started working on my novel. If they wanted to act like children, I could as well. Fifteen minutes passed before someone spoke. I was curious who would break first. Honestly, my bet was on Bryant. Dakota hit the bars. "This guy, Arielle? Seriously?"

I glanced up at him for a split second, face unchanged, and then went back to typing. Bryant sighed. "Look, it got out of hand. We were just talking, and it escalated. I do not want you to see me any differently, Ari." Bryant's eyes were filled with remorse. He definitely was still feeling it from when I left his place abruptly.

My eyes rolled to the back of my head. "First of all, stop calling me that. It's weird. Second of all, I don't know why you were fighting. I am not dating either one of you anymore." Dakota would no longer make eye contact with me, and Bryant looked like he got punched in the face, which was tempting.

Dakota spoke next. "I overreacted the other day. We aren't exclusive, but I was caught off guard." His eyes went from anger to sadness. The officer came back to check on me.

"Look, I am not looking for anything serious right now. We just met. I am not stopping you from dating anyone else."

"I have no interest in doing that," Bryant jumped in.

"Same here." Dakota leaned his head on one of the bars.

"No, not you! I heard you on the phone the other day. I know what you're doing." Tears welled in my eyes; my attempt to mentally force them away was barely enough to keep them at bay.

"The phone? Wait, is that why you took off? My phone conversation with my business partner?" He let out a small chuckle and leaned against the bars, similar to Dakota. "Ari—sorry, Arielle... we were talking about a client that we need to control. This woman is a CEO of her own company, but she is ruining the PR of the business because she is a night club lush in her forties." He continued to reminisce of his conversation, and I started to believe him. Whether it was the truth or he was a good storyteller, I wanted to believe him. Turning back to the officer, I asked, "What is it going to take to get them released early?"

Her eyebrows went up. "You sure?"

I nodded. Dakota and Bryant wrote me two checks when we got outside because of the public disturbance on a main road. It was only five hundred dollars. Once they handed me the checks, the awkwardness of the situation caught up to us. Eye contact was avoided, and I turned to walk away. "Arielle," they said in unison. They both glared at each other with frustration—a reminder they were and are in competition. They were hot, but I don't think it was worth the drama. I had enough going on right now. I turned back around and waved as I continued walking. "I'll text you," I said as cold as I could. I needed space, and I did not want to give either of them the impression any of these relationships would be long-lasting, despite my temporary desire every once in a while.

My front door was locked, and I left my key inside, so I walked around to the back and went through the sliding glass doors. I knew they had to be unlocked since Ben was still crashing in my spare bedroom. I missed my sister being here instead. She was fun, while he was annoying. I had hoped he would be leaving, and I considered bringing it up today. Despite it only being two in the afternoon, I took a shot of rum followed by another and another. "Whoa, killer, slow down, will you?" I glanced up at him as Ben entered the room with a grin on his face.

"I would rather not, thanks." I opened the fridge to pull out a beer, and I popped the cap off.

"You look like you had a rough morning." He came around the counter, his breath smelling like peppermint, and his eyes were narrowed in on me. I tried to take a step back as I started chugging my beer. He slid his hand behind my back quickly but pulled me in slowly. His face came close to mine, and I tilted my head the opposite way to avoid it. The shots I took were hitting me pretty hard. I looked at the rum bottle. "What the fu—"

"Is it good? I added something to it to help you relax."

My eyes were starting to close. Exhaustion rushed over me, and it felt like the more I tried to stay awake, the more tired I became. "Ben, no..." I pushed away and stumbled, falling to the ground hard. I grabbed the countertop with one hand, hoping to push off the ground, but instead a fist landed on me hard.

"I am really sick of you choosing everyone but me. I am great, much better than those losers you were doing after I worked so hard to make sure you thought your ex was cheating on you." I couldn't get the words out. My mouth was numb, and my head was spinning. "Yes, that's right. Your ex didn't really cheat on you. I mean…don't get me wrong. Once you left, he moved on quickly. I saved you. I saved you from him. This is the thanks I get?" He looked crazy, no longer like the Ben I knew. He knelt down on one knee, caressing my face. I was becoming cross-eyed. I bit his hand as hard as I could manage. "Ouch!" He pulled his hand away, and no sooner than that did it come back and hit me across the face. Darkness.

Voices. There were two—no, that can't be…one? One person talking to himself? No, that just couldn't be right. I could hear, but my sight had not kicked in. "Move her to the bed."

"No way, that crazy bitch bit me!"

"You shouldn't have touched her, anyway. We had an agreement, you idiot."

"Is she waking up?"

I heard footsteps. "Not for long." Liquid poured down my mouth again; it was pungent. I could hear Kira barking; it was muffled and distant.

My eyes opened first, the feeling in my body came an eternity later. I tried to swing my legs out of bed, but my body felt like it got hit by a truck. The windows were opened, and light streamed in. I could smell puke. It must have been in my hair. Glancing down, I noticed it was all over my clothes, and some even got on my bed. Trying to talk but my mouth feeling like sandpaper, I eased out of bed, but every move made me want to die. I went for the bathroom but stopped in the hallway. What was I forgetting? When I caught a look at myself in the mirror, my hair looked like a rat's nest that was built up over twenty years. The memories flooded back. I looked down, not really knowing what all had happened. Panic filled me, making it near impossible to breathe. I slammed the door shut, locking it, and hopped in the shower. Tears streamed down my face. I felt dirty, although I was not sure what happened. I knew what could have happened…assuming it didn't. Did it? I scrubbed every inch of my body and shampooed my hair five, maybe six times. I could hear my phone ringing from my room. It just wasn't worth the rush. Was he still here? Turning off the shower, I eased out of it, trying to be as quiet as I could for no reason other than fear. If he was here, he would know I was awake because of the shower, but being quiet seemed like the right thing to do. Opening the door slightly, I peeked out, feeling very much like my seven-year-old self sneaking out of bed to get a cinnamon roll in the middle of the night. I heard nothing. Tiptoeing down the hall, I looked around. There were no lights on, no TV or music. The waves crashing in was the only sound being made; everything else stands still. "Hell...hello?" Peeking around every corner, there was no one here, no one at all. Suddenly, I was grateful for my small beach cottage, as it had no hiding spots. The door to the quest bedroom was open; the sunlight streamed through every window. Ben was gone; there was no trace of him, as if he was never here. My phone started ringing again. I let it. I paced up and down the hall, avoiding the kitchen at all costs. In the bathroom, I didn't look at my face. Lifting it was hard enough, let alone processing anything. The mirror in the hall was unavoidable; there was a crater-sized bruise surrounding my eye, and small bruises lined my arm. The headache was easing up; the rest of my body felt nothing. Kira lay by the back door asleep, as if everything was normal.

An hour later, I was at the hospital getting checked. The nurses were nice, but I desperately wanted to hear good news. It was kind of sad, considering getting punched out and drugged good news over the alternative. "Taylor? Arielle Taylor?"

Looking up, I said, "Yes?" Time seemed to slow again. I just wanted her to spit it out.

The nurse was short, shorter than me, at least, with hair that curled around her face and reminded me of a grandmother figure—not mine because I never knew mine, but the typical granny everyone else typically has. "You had a very bad night, but you were not raped."

I breathed a sigh of relief. Tears flooded down my face, and for a split second, I considered praying. Another hour passed while they tried giving me various pamphlets and pushing me in the direction of counselors, but I refused. My phone was put on silent the second I stepped out my front door. My sister had finally started returning my calls, but now was not the time. My phone started to vibrate as I walked out of the hospital. I pulled it out of my pocket. It was Marcie. Wow, what impeccable timing. "Hello?" My tone was flat.

"What the fuck did you do?" Her voice was angry, but there was a small hint of worry.

I laughed in disbelief. "What do you mean what the fuck did I do?"

"You and Ben, he called me and told me what happened." Suddenly, Marcie was no longer my friend or publisher; she was a jealous ex-girlfriend with the wrong idea of the truth.

"Marce, I don't know what Ben told you, but I would bet my life it is not correct."

"You should not have done that, Ari, you promised. You're going to regret this." She hung up the phone, and in that second, I contacted human resources via e-mail. I wanted to scream and throw everything and anything. Heading back home to get Kira and take her for a walk, I desperately wanted a drink, but the idea of attempting it made me nauseous. As I passed people, heading to my car, I could feel people trying not to stare at my bruise. With every purposefully avoided stare, my pain and sadness slowly began turning into anger. I could feel it with every bone in my body slowly building it from my toes to the bruise on my face. This was not how I would end.

Kira was happy to see me, and she was about the only being I would tolerate right now. Dakota and Bryant had taken a step back. I almost wished they hadn't; maybe they would have been there. I couldn't sit here thinking about what could have been, but it was hard to not believe Ben was not behind everything entirely. It all made sense. I called the sheriff; they sent a female cop to the house to take a statement and to look at the kitchen. Pressing charges was the last thing on my mind this morning. She inspected every inch though and asked if I knew Marcie, and I did, she would do whatever she needed to exact revenge for nothing. When Marcie and I met, it seemed like a great match. She was driven and passionate about publishing. She pitched my first book and gave me hope, but behind that kindness and the motivation she provided to me, there was darkness with it. I just never expected to be at the opposite end of her fury, not until Ben started having feelings for me. Things change quickly no matter where you are.

"Maybe a different house?"

"That would be best, assuming Ben is caught. Otherwise there is no point." I felt as if I was lying to him. Nowhere felt safe, and sure, knowing my tormentor was one thing, but catching him was another. "What I don't understand is why he went through all the unnecessary trouble of sending me things via e-mail and coming here directly. I don't even know if I have been having dreams or blackouts."

Dakota was sprawled out on the couch, shirt raised a little over his waist, hair ruffled, and feet on the side of the couch. "Did you give your medications to the sheriff's department for testing with their crime unit?"

I shook my head. After telling the police about the blackouts and visions, they requested my medications to have the lab test them to see if he was drugging me like he did the rum. I was almost hoping he did so I would know I was not crazy, but either way I felt helpless. "If it means anything, I want you to stay. You could even stay with me."

Hope. That was what I saw when I looked at Dakota. I liked him, but when he turned on me so quickly, it pushed me away a bit. He was right though. Dating two guys seemed wrong to me, but I was raised conservatively, despite that having changed now as an adult. I just felt weird about it. At this point I should be further along in either relationship, but I came here to focus on me, not on my heart. Not that I love either of them now, but I could see it happening. For a brief second, I considered asking Dakota to leave, but what point would that serve?

"No, I don't think that is the best idea. I appreciate the offer though. My realtor is looking for another place for me in the area. I don't even care if it is close." My words had an unintended effect on him; he was hurt at me wanting to leave without a doubt, but I couldn't care. Right now, I needed to focus on staying alive and writing a novel. Which one would be successful I was not entirely sure. The bruise on my face was my current defining feature; luckily I did not have to leave the house because everything I needed could be delivered here. Dakota started to fall asleep; he had been going back and forth to his jobs and coming here as soon as he could. I didn't blame him. I opened my laptop and typed away despite the desperate need to lock myself in the bathroom with a kitchen knife for the rest of my life.

The sound of glass breaking woke me out of my zen. "What the fuck!" I jumped out of my chair, waking Dakota up with my voice, and he jumped up immediately.

"What, what?" Looking around frantically, I noticed a small glass figurine I had on a small table by the window shattered on the floor. The small figurine was a blue-and-purple glass sea turtle. I thought they were precious and found it in a thrift shop along the coast shortly after moving in. Dakota eased up and grabbed a broom from the kitchen closet.

"Of course, everything I love falls to pieces," I mumbled to myself. Whether or not Dakota heard me was unclear because he didn't say a word.

"Maybe this is too forward, but you need to relax a bit."

I scoffed, "Easier said than done." Dakota walked down the hall and into the bathroom without saying a word. I heard the sound of water, so he must have turned on the bath. I watched him cross from the bathroom to my room carrying the speaker I had by my bed and then back into the bathroom. I stood at the end of the hall with my throw blanket wrapped around me. My muscles were tense, and a bath seemed like a good idea. As a child, when I felt anxious, I would take a bubble bath and read. It helped me forget the challenges of being around my mother and, often, being ridiculed by the other kids in school. The last time I took a bath at Bryant's, but that was a strange experience, one I actually have not thought of much recently. Perhaps it was not something I should discredit. The paranoia was coming back, but it didn't feel like paranoia. I was wide awake, and I fell asleep right after having a small glass of wine or a bottle… I remember the bottle being empty when I woke up, but I don't even remember finishing the glass I actually poured. "Arielle? Hello?" Dakota stood in front of me, his hands on both of my shoulders.

"Hey, what, sorry." Everything came back into view.

"I ran a bath for you, tossed in one of those smelly balls for baths, whatever they are called, and there is a bottle of water on the counter. Relax, and I will be out here making sure you are safe."

Tears welled up in my eyes, but they didn't get further than that. Heading to the bathroom, for a split second, I felt calm, and the closer I got to the bathroom, the more I could smell warmth and lavender. I glanced back at Dakota, who was plopping down on the couch with a beer in his hand, the TV flicked on.

Twenty minutes in, my eyes started to drop. Silence was my best friend, aside from the muffled sounds of the TV coming from down the hall. I slipped farther into the water, which was surprisingly still warm. A loud crash resounded through the house, sounding like glass shattering in the living room. It jolted me out of my peace and quiet. I sloshed around in the bath water before I became still, hoping to hear Dakota say he dropped something. Yelling reverberated down the hall, hearing only muffled sounds; I knew it was Dakota. I jumped out of the tub and threw my clothes on from before. My hair was dripping wet from the tub. Whipping out my cell phone, I dialed 911 but nothing went through. The signal was jammed. I slid over to the small bathroom window facing the front of the house. The cop must still be out there, watching the place. The cop car was out front and the lights were on, but the door was open. An arm dangled out of it. "Oh, for fuck's sake!" I whispered to myself. The sound of my living room getting demolished continued.

He was going to find me; there was nowhere to run. What about Dakota? I needed to get to him; maybe together he could overpower this psychopath. I opened the door slowly, not fully convinced of my newfound bravery. Just as I was able to open the door, without turning to face the living room, a sliver of silver flew past my head and hit the closet door at the end of the hallway. Turning to look at it, I saw a large knife stood in the middle of the door, not wavering in the least, and my head whipped around to look at the expert knife thrower. He stood in the living room, dressed in black with his face covered by a white mask. His head rolled from side to side as if he was getting adjusted for whatever was going to come next. My blood was bubbling, and fear shook me. I would not survive this. Neither one of us moved for an eternity; time seemed to slow in my final moments. I was closer to the knife. I could not see him holding any other weapon, but if given the chance, he could overpower me just with strength. My feet were wet; if I ran to the knife, I'll slip, maybe. His head stopped moving. "That's not a good sign," I mumbled and took off toward the knife, slamming into the hallway as his footsteps slammed on the floor toward me. Yanking the knife out of the wall took two tries, but with that final pull, it slid out. I flung it around as he approached me. Seeing the knife he slid, stopping as soon as he could. I was right; he held no other weapon.

His eyes were visible through the mask. Blue. He stood five feet away from me, watching me like I was some animal at the zoo. Was he amused by my fight?

"What do you want from me? What do you want?" Unsuccessfully holding a steady tone, my voice cracked at the end. His eyes didn't blink, and he didn't move a step.

When another voice sounded from behind his mask, I shook. "I…want you."

"Ben, I am sorry I turned you down, but this is excessive," I said, trying to ease the tension. My blood pressure was high, and the hair on my arms were standing straight up.

He sighed. "I'm not Ben. That fool didn't deserve you!" His anger erupted.

"I know, I turned him down."

He took a step forward, the knife still pointed in his direction. "And I am so proud of you for that. However, it doesn't make up for what you did!"

"What I did? What did I do?" The knife started to wobble in my hand. He could tell and took another step.

"We could have been great together. I would have done anything for you."

A single tear fell down my face. "I don't even know who you are!"

He went to take another step but stopped. A moan came from the living room. Dakota slowly rose from behind the couch, phone in hand. His blood was everywhere, and his face was covered in it. "The police...are...on their way...," he said as he fell to the ground. Sirens sounded in the background.

My imagination must have been playing a trick on me because in that moment, my attempted murderer sighed out of annoyance. "Okay, that is frustrating. Look, Arielle, you're going to die. I am telling you this because I love you and always have. Tonight isn't the night though." He pushed me up against the wall and grabbed the knife like it was candy. In one swift movement he slashed it across my face. "Ahhh!" The blood dripped down me faster than the tear from earlier.

He whispered in my ear, "Something to remember me by," and he took off down the hall and out the back just as the front door busted open.

Focus on breathing, focus on breathing. I crumbled to the ground as cops flooded my home. My home. It wasn't that anymore, but I wanted to take it back. The paramedics rushed into the living room. What they were doing to Dakota I was not sure, but they were the experts, not me. Panic had been a constant state for me for several weeks, but now, I felt nothing. Sirens whirled in the background, and a few officers swept the house while paramedics moved Dakota to the ambulance. All that noise started to fade. Sitting at the end of the hallway, I could see everything happening, but I no longer felt present. A female officer knelt in front of me asking me my name repeatedly. I knew it, but nothing came out. "Miss...hello, miss?" Both of her arms were on my shoulders lightly shaking me; it almost pulled me out of my funk, but all I could see was the devil standing in front of me with my life in his hands.

CHAPTER 10

THE PHONE RANG SEVERAL TIMES, EACH TIME FORCING ME INTO THE VOICE MAIL
pit of doom. I had not talked to Bryant in days, and I needed him
now more than ever. The guilt consumed me of how I suspected
him of foul play with my heart and mind. I didn't know who Ben
was working with, but it couldn't be Bryant, and now I know for
sure it was not Dakota. He finally made it out of surgery, but the
time I was able to see him, he was already gone and had not said a
word to me. I couldn't blame him; it was my fault he was attacked
and almost died. "Bryant, I don't know if you are on another business trip, but I need you. Please call me back." Another voice
mail, which sounded like the other ten I had already left. I was no
stranger to paranoia at this point, and the guilt I would have had
for blowing him up and acting needy was overridden by my fear. I
grabbed all my belongings and packed up. I found a beach condo
down the road that held three apartments, and mine was at the
very top. The movers had my stuff in within three hours. I still had
the beach view, but the serenity I had when I first moved here was
all but gone. The only comfort I had left was knowing I was on the
third floor of a very oddly designed apartment. Each apartment
had two floors, so technically the building had six floors. Once
I regained consciousness at my old house, I called my sister, and
in turn she contacted my realtor and threatened her to find me
another place or she will post all over social media about the inci-
dent and how the realtor company did nothing to accommodate

me. Granted, in most cases, it was an abrupt approach I would not have allowed, but in this case, I was sincerely grateful.

Walking up four flights of stairs was exhausting but also promising, and to get to my floor a special key card was needed. After using the keycard, there was another door which led to the apartment. The entire place was modern—concrete floors and countertops, brand-new appliances, and huge windows spanning from floor to ceiling. It was basically the exact opposite of my first home, and I could not be more thrilled. The first floor held the kitchen, living room, a bathroom, and access to the first patio, which had a hot tub. The second floor was connected to the living room via a spiral metal staircase, which looked odd compared to the cement. The second floor held one bedroom and another bathroom. It was more of a loft, but it also had access to a second patio, which had its own built-in firepit. I locked both front doors and checked the patio access from both sides. There was no getting in unexpectedly. I called the security guy who had helped me previously. The installations for my apartment took two more hours. The bruise on my face had been replaced by the knife scratch that would more than likely become a scar. A giant bandage covered the side of my face. I felt like a bad guy in a crappy action movie.

"What am I doing here?" Kira stared at me, not that she could answer my question. She picked up her toy alligator with the squeaker and carried it over to the couch, throwing it up in the air a few times before laying her head on it and falling asleep. My phone rang, playing AC/DC's "Back in Black." I picked it up after an eternity. "Hello?"

"Hi, Ms. Taylor, this is Clara with Sigma Publishing. I wanted to give you a call to let you know I am now your contact, as Marcie Johnson has now left the company."

I scoffed. "Good riddance. Thank you for giving me a call, Clara."

"Of course, of course, I am a big fan, and I am looking forward to working with you. On that note, I do have to ask, how close are you to finishing the novel?"

The rage that erupted inside of me could not be explained in a few words; any and all niceties went out the window in a matter of seconds. "Are you fucking kidding me right now? I have been gone barely two months to work on this novel. Your company has been driving me up the wall about something that I typically spend six months on. The book comes first, the film comes second—that is how I see it! Furthermore, you do understand why Marcie is no longer with the company and the inappropriate behavior from Ben. So the fact that you dare try to push me to finish the novel any sooner is amazing to me."

"Ms. Taylor, I apologize."

"I will contact you if and when it is done before the date mentioned on my contract." If I could slam a cell phone, I would, but frankly that was one less broken item I needed to be dealing with right now. Kira popped her head up over the couch. "It's okay, I'm fine." And with that she fell back asleep. My guard dog was more of a cuddle dog at this point.

At two in the morning, I woke up, as if I was jerked awake. I sat up quickly and scanned the room. Flipping the light on, I saw nothing. I removed the baseball bat from under my pillow and jumped from the bed, glancing underneath in case my own personal boogeyman waited for me farther into the darkness. Something felt wrong, but everything seemed right. Bat in hand, I inspected the bathroom and the stairs leading to the first floor. From the top of the stairs, I could see everything except the extra bathroom and the entire patio. Slowly descending the stairs, I felt ready—ready for whatever came my way, but not without a little fear. My friends died because of me. I would not die because of some psychopath, whoever it was. After examining the first floor, I relaxed a bit and dropped the bat from my shoulders to the floor. Wait…my closet! "Holy shit!" I grabbed the bat from the floor and turned around to see a figure at the top of the stairs. "How the hell did you get in here?"

The figure slowly descended the stairs; with every step my heart beat faster. "I was given a key. It's amazing how accommodating your realtor was. All I had to do was call her and tell her I was your sister."

"What? Impossible! She has my sister's contact information. She would know it wasn't her!" I took a step back with every step my intruder took. This one had a female voice. The last one I dealt with was a male; how many people were trying to kill me now?

"No, that was me. Your sister is no longer in the game."

Her voice sounded familiar, but I couldn't place it. Marcie? "Marcie? Is that you?" She descended the final step and removed her mask, her red curly hair puffed out of the black mask. "Are you kidding me right now? All this for him?" Ben had this bitch wrapped around his finger, and now she was trying to kill me. Perfect. "Shouldn't you be happy I turned him down? He is all yours, I want nothing to do with him."

She slowly unsheathed a knife, twisting it slowly on her finger. "I want him to be happy, and unfortunately, you make him happy. Besides killing you is a plus, then I won't have to see your face or hear your name anymore."

I stepped around the kitchen table, bat raised by my head. "Where, might I ask, is your demented boyfriend? Hmm? Licking his wounds in a corner I suppose?"

She stopped, and her mouth twitched. Making her angrier seemed like a bad idea, but I couldn't help myself. "He's taking care of some loose ends."

Suddenly her comment about Amberley hit me. "What did you mean about Amberley? Where is she?" Desperation leaked from my voice. Trying to hold it together, I had no choice but to confirm my weak spot. Marcie threw her head back laughing; cackling would be more accurate, but that was only because she looked like a witch in her all-black outfit.

"Dead, well…let's see. Amby? Are you still here?" I looked around, and my face fell flat at the top of the stairs. A hand was visible from the hallway, but it was covered in blood. My sister's face came into view, which was as bloody as her hand, if not worse. "Ari, run." Her words came out in a gravelly whisper. Her head dropped, and her arm went limp. "No! No!" My sobs came out choked.

Marcie lunged toward me. "No! I did not hide in that closet with your drugged-up sister for hours waiting for you to run away. If you want to be with her, make this easy."

Marcie ran at me with the knife. I swung the bat and hit her wrist; the knife flew to the floor several steps away. I swung the bat again into her head as hard as I could, and she toppled over. "Timber, bitch." I ran up the stairs to check on Amberley, scrambling to check her wrist and her neck. No pulse. "Fuck, I'm terrible at this. She can't be dead. No, no, no!" I rushed over to my side table and grabbed my cell phone. By the time I made it back to the top of the stairs, Marcie's body was gone.

Amberley was confirmed dead on the scene. Police officers and paramedics were there but proved to be useless, time and time again actually. The paramedics rolled my sister's lifeless corpse out of the apartment. The cops and the sheriff approached me to give a statement. I walked over to a hanging frame centered on the wall by the stairs; it was the only frame hung there and for a reason. The frame was a fake. I swung it open to reveal a monitor set with a recorder. I had the security company install one immediately after moving in. I popped out the CD and handed it to the sheriff without saying a word. "Ms. Taylor, we would like to hear from you directly what happened," one of the cops said to me. He was young or at least younger than the rest. He was blond with blue eyes and looked like he should be modeling, not investigating a murder and break-in.

"You have what you need. Get out." I walked over to the door and stood with it open until they filed out in a single line in silence. They knew I had no energy to deal with them just as much as Marcie and Ben. What I failed to understand was who the third guy was, unless it was Ben who was just lying to me. I kicked everyone out before the clean-up crew could arrive. From under the sink, I grabbed a bottle of bleach and several towels. I would clean it my damn self, the blood of my sister, my best friend.

Her blood was on my hands already, at least in theory, so it might as well be on them literally.

Despite wearing gloves, I could feel the blood seeping in, not literally but almost as if it was consuming me. I felt like I was just pushing her blood around, my blood. I poured the bottle of bleach on the entire floor; I might as well have put it in the sprinkler system. After what felt like hours of bleaching and sobbing uncontrollably, I needed rest, but I couldn't. My body was willing, but my mind was incapable of shutting down, at least enough to get sleep. How do you sleep when your sister was murdered in front of you? Slowly walking into my room, I crumbled to the floor. "Why? Why did you leave me?" The words bellowed out as if I had no control. It wasn't her fault; it was mine. I ran over to my bookshelf and flung everything off. Knickknacks and frames came hurtling to the floor, and glass spread everywhere. Kira ran out of the room and down the stairs swiftly. My phone rang. It was Bryant, but I didn't care. It rang for eternity; the ridiculous tone I chose last year mocked me now. Funny how something as simple as a ringtone could remind you of simpler times, happier ones, one where my sister was alive. Screams erupted from my body; the anger boiling in my blood gave me a headache. I barely made it to the bathroom and puked my guts out. The strain it put on my body caused immediate soreness. I hung my head low. My hair, which was a knotted mess, nearly fell in the toilet. I pulled it up in a bun, and it finally stayed put. Moving sounded painful, but so did doing nothing. The scene replayed in my head, haunting every synapse and every other piece of me. I let the cops call my parents. I had no desire to talk to them. Hell…I could barely keep myself together, and I knew they would blame me. My eyes closed, but I would not call what I received as sleep.

CHAPTER 11

"Arielle! Arielle!" yelling and banging came from the front door. I was not sure how that was possible, but I gave up trying to figure things out. No one would leave me alone, not the publishing company or my new editor, not even the cops. After two days of being cooped up in the apartment without food, it seemed necessary to get something, but if I left and they came back, then what? I was afraid to leave, and I was afraid to stay, but staying seemed like a lot less effort. "Ugh, what time is it?" I mumbled to myself and crawled out of bed. I picked up my phone that was lying on the floor by my bedroom door. Dead. "Yeah, that makes sense," I said as I headed downstairs. The clock on the microwave showed two o'clock. Based on the light outside, I assumed it was the afternoon. I grabbed the bat I had by the door, swinging it around my shoulder. I peered through the peephole. Bryant. "Hmmm, imagine that."

I opened the door, and he rushed in, picking me up in a giant hug and holding it for an eternity. He set me back down, and I stared at him, watching to see what would happen next. I looked the part of a lunatic from a mental institution for sure. I wore a big baggy blue shirt with gray sweatpants. My hair was greasy and in a ponytail, and I couldn't remember the last time I brushed my teeth. "Arielle, I am so sorry I have not been here. I promise no more business trips, I swear! I am incredibly sorry about your sister. I can't even believe this."

"Well, believe it." I would have been happy to see him at any other point in time, but this time, today, I felt nothing. Numb. The thought of smiling for even a split second made me sick to my stomach. I did not deserve to be happy, which was a thought that I had replayed in my head for two days around the clock—at least the times I'd been awake and sober. The kitchen was flooded with various liquor bottles and beer. Some empty and others spilled over.

"What is going on here?" He looked around in disbelief but not disgust, which was appreciated. I turned my back on him and trudged back up the stairs to crawl in bed; I had not touched the novel in days, and I truly could not care less. I heard Bryant on his phone for a few minutes before he followed me up, pulling me out of bed. "Come on, let's go. Time to shower."

I groaned. I would have punched him in the face, but that would be exerting too much effort for what I would expect to be no results. "I know, I know. It'll help…temporarily, though." He stripped me and himself and then helped me into the shower.

I had no interest in standing; it was too painful. Life itself was too painful. "I should just let them kill me."

Bryant spun me around to face him; the hot water ran down my back, and it felt good. "Don't you ever say that! Do you hear me? I am serious, Arielle. You are a fighter, so fight, goddamn it!" Tears sprung to my face, but they crawled down my face quietly as I nodded. He let me lean into his chest as he shampooed my hair. After several minutes I added conditioner and stood facing the water for a bit longer. If only the water could wash away my sins, but this was real life, so I gave up on that idea. The steam lifted the excruciating pain out of me, if even for a few minutes. I cried on and off, probably looking like a maniac, but Bryant stayed and rubbed my back. He was kind, caring, and I couldn't even imagine how I thought he could be involved in this. I started to take a few breaths and let the hot water take me in. After about twenty or so minutes, we got out, and Bryant wrapped me in a giant fluffy towel, one I didn't even know I had. Kira waited by the door, almost as if she was my security dog, and ran into her bed with one of her toys. She nested for a bit, which usually made me laugh, and plopped

CHAPTER 9

I HAD NOT HEARD FROM BEN, AND BECAUSE OF THIS, FEAR FOLLOWED ME EVERY-where. I was not afraid of him really but more of the person he became without me knowing. I think what scared me the most was knowing there was someone else in my house, and I have no idea who that could be. I had called Dakota and Bryant to tell them what had happened. Dakota rushed over, but Bryant was in Michigan for the weekend for some conference. I refused every call from my sister and directed my focus to communicating with human resources. I had sent them the report from the sheriff's office and proof of my hospital visit. To my knowledge, Ben was being terminated. That helped a bit, but no one had been able to find him. Dakota sat down on the couch, several feet from me, and I was curled up into the chair with a throw blanket. "I'm cursed," I mumbled into my blanket, wondering how my paradise took such a quick tumble and the fairytale relationships turned into a fight to the death with a side of trust issues. Paranoia swept over me in the last two weeks, and I did not wear it well. Bags hung from my eyes. I was trying a new positive approach, but it was fleeting.

"Are you thinking of leaving for good?" Dakota watched me, as if I would unravel right in front of him. A moment of silence passed as I stared off into space. Possibly—how do I answer this without sounding like a whiney little brat?

"I love this place, but this particular location has so many bad memories. How could I stay?"

down, her butt landing on her squeaky toy and setting it off. A smile escaped me as she jumped up and barked at it, but it quickly vanished. "How am I going to get through this?" I threw a pillow off the bed and crawled in.

"We," he stressed, "will make it through this one day at a time." Sleep came quickly; turned out misery was a great sleep aid.

Waking up the next day to Bryant snoring next to me was almost comforting. Kira made her way back up on the bed, and my legs were wrapped around her so I could fit. The police called to tell me they found a woman who matched Marcie's description fifteen miles up the coast, and they would call me back with more details. "There is something else you need to know." The sheriff was silent for an eternity.

"What's that?"

"Dakota Lawrence is missing. After he was brought to the hospital, he has not been seen. Actually, no one confirmed he ever made it to the hospital."

I could feel my head spinning. "The paramedics took him away, we watched them take him away!" My voice became shrill, reminding me of my mother.

"Yes, I remember, but for some reason, he never made it to the hospital, and we have been unable to track the bus that took him." I stepped out of my bedroom to take the call to not wake up Bryant, but I was louder than I thought, or rather, my barely furnished apartment still had some echo to it. Bryant was walking down the stairs with Kira by his side. Wiping the sleep out of his eyes, he almost missed the last step. "Any word?"

"No, nothing confirmed, but they said they would get back to me as soon as they could." There was a knock on my door before I could take back the lie. Should I tell him about Dakota? Bryant and I held still, waiting for another knock or for silence in general. The sound woke us up from the last bit of silence we were able to capture.

"Arielle, I'll get it." I could feel the panic coming back; it nearly knocked the wind out of me. Heat rose in my chest, but that could have been nausea. Bryant grabbed the baseball bat by the front door, peered through the peephole, and swung it open, jumping out with the bat. There was no one there. He double-checked both sides and even peered down the steps.

"Bryant, what is that?" I took a few steps forward but stopped. There was a medium-sized manila envelope on the ground outside my door.

Bryant picked it up and brought it inside. "Whatever is in here isn't that large." He opened the envelope and dumped the contents on the counter. I couldn't say what happened first, the scream or the puke. Bryant jumped away. "Holy shit!" There was a human finger on my counter. I puked on the floor, and Kira started barking out of concern. Dakota! Oh god, please don't be from Dakota. Bryant picked up the phone and dialed the cops, where they mentioned everything I was previously told. Bryant did not give me hell for not telling him; in fact he didn't even mention it.

It felt like a routine. For the next three days, around noon, when there was the most traffic everywhere in town, there was a knock on my door and another envelope. Sometimes it would be a finger or a lock of hair, but who they belonged to, I had no idea... or rather who they had belonged to. We were used to it by the second day. I stopped writing. I was done for now. Even Bryant's positive attitude was starting to deflate; it was hard to keep it going when you had five random digits waving at us and mocking the last bit of sanity we hoped to have.

"I see no point in this. For real, I am a writer. I should not be getting this much fucking attention!" I took the baseball bat to the counter, and Bryant slid over on his socks, grabbing the baseball bat from my hands and tossing it at the couch. It landed perfectly, and Kira lunged for it. He grabbed my arms and took in a slow breath. I mocked him because I knew he wanted me to relax as best as I could. I was past scared, but I was furious. "I need a gun."

"Oh really? Well...I guess that isn't a bad idea, but I have a new fear—you'll shoot me instead!"

That got a quick chuckle from me, one of the few I have been able to spare in a long time. "I need protection, and you won't always be around. You'll eventually have to go back to work." He turned around to grab two cups of hot liquid, one was coffee for him and the other was probably green tea for me. We stepped out onto the patio.

"I know, and it's a good idea, but no offense, you'll have to work on your impulse control."

I feigned offense. "First of all, I can handle a gun, and if you are so worried about getting shot, you can stand beside me!"

His eyes widened in amusement. "Oh really? Now you are a big badass? Fascinating, this should be fun." He chuckled as Kira ran up to him and forced him to pet her. So much for an aggressive dog. At least she was good company. "So, Ms. Badass, what do you say about venturing out of the apartment for a day? You've been cooped up in here too long, and even I am getting stir-crazy."

I felt bad for a minute. He had been so nice keeping me company, but I had refused to leave even though this place had been proven not to be any safer than outside. "Yeah, you are probably right. I was down for anything at this point, but getting out was a good idea." I jumped up to get dressed.

"Oh, right now?" A hint of surprise escaped his voice.

"Why not?" I knew I was not a badass by any means, but everyone was getting hurt, and I only had Bryant now. I didn't know if he could take care of himself, but I could not run the risk. So far everyone I cared about had been murdered or was missing. He watched me, as if I were fragile, and I was, but I did not have the luxury of being that anymore.

"Do we need to talk about him?" he asked, as if those words were not loaded enough. Was I really going to talk to Bryant about the other guy? I couldn't even do that with Dakota, but Bryant had always been slightly more understanding.

"I don't know." My hesitation was clear on several layers.

"I know this is awkward, but I care about you and you care about both of us. I love you." Those words that meant so much, they carried weight, and looking into Bryant's eyes, I could tell he believed he meant it. However, I did not feel the same, I think. I couldn't be in love with two guys, could I? My nose scrunched up in thought. I had not had any time to seriously think about my relationships with these guys. I couldn't say it back and get his hopes up, but if I said nothing, then what? I guess my stunned silence provided the answer I was unwilling to give. He gave me a hug, and I could almost feel the hurt radiating through him, but he said nothing. I pulled away because my silence was not enough of a slap in the face. I grabbed a bottle of wine as another knock came on the door. More police came in to gather the evidence. Every finger seemed a little different in size. "Dakota," I whispered as the crime scene unit picked up the finger. Could it be his? I remembered his blue eyes, staring back at me with kindness, and his sexy brown hair styled up. He had a smile that lit up a room and made me feel things I didn't know were possible. Here I was thinking of him as if he were already dead. Then again…he very well might be.

There were still no leads on who Ben and Marcie could be working with. The police were baffled that these two could disappear without a trace but pop up undetected whenever they desired. They checked street cameras, monitored their social media webpages, and were in constant contact with their families. I overheard a rookie cop foolishly announce he was shocked I was still alive. This was a game of cat and mouse, but it was a gang of cats and a very tiny mouse. My dreams of the unknown accomplice continued to haunt me, if it even truly happened. My sanity had been called into question, and I very well might be one more attack away from being forced to see a therapist. Until then I would continue to refuse. My phone was ringing off the hook from various family members and the publishing company. I started blocking numbers left and right. I even considered shutting off my phone at this point. Everyone who got close to me would get murdered, and if these psychopaths had anything to do with it, I would also die alone. As supportive as Bryant had been, I needed to do this on my own. I watched Bryant; he was sleeping on the couch in the upright position with a beer in his hand. The five-o'clock shadow he was flaunting made him even more pleasant to look at, instead of a hobo like most men. He held a baseball bat in the other hand. A smirk flashed across my face at the hilarity of the situation. I had known him for a few weeks, and he, of some reason, had not been scared off yet, which was nice but made me feel slightly guilty. If the roles were reversed, I would have been gone ages ago. Kira laid at my feet and occasionally would stick her tongue out to lick them. "Would you stop? That tickles!" One eye opened and looked right at me and proceeded to flutter closed. A second later, his tongue was out again, just resting on my foot. Opening my laptop to check my e-mails, I noticed the webcam light was on. "That's weird." I checked my browser to make sure that I didn't have an old chat open, but my computer was bare. A message popped up on my screen: "Trust no one, get out—D." Dakota? I frantically looked around me. The paranoia I once held came back. I didn't hear anything unusual, and Bryant was still asleep. This had to be a trap. If I left, I would die, but if I stayed...I might also die. There was no escape, but if I could save him—Bryant, that is—then maybe it would be worth it. I couldn't continue to let other people die for me, and for what? Sprinting up the stairs, I quickly changed into black leggings and a gray sweatshirt and tossed on my sneakers. Throwing my hair in a ponytail, I settled on a green ball cap I had received randomly from one of the bookstores that I did a book signing a few years ago. Kira watched me ruefully, as if she knew what my plan was. She picked up her gator toy and brought it over to me, setting it by my feet. Bryant would take care of her, I know he would.

Dear Bryant,

I'm so sorry. Words cannot express how painful leaving is, so many good people have died because of me, and I cannot let you be a victim too. I appreciate everything you have done for me. Our time together has been special. Please understand why I am doing this. I don't know what is going to happen, but I know I will not be back. I am seeking out the monsters who are doing this to me, and I am going to end it. It needs to end. Please keep watch over Kira for me. She is a good girl and deserves a good home.

Yours truly,
Arielle

The beach was quiet. For a small town, I felt I would eventually not be surprised by this, but considering how beautiful it was, I don't think my mindset would ever change. What is it about serenity that makes someone nostalgic? I made sure to get as far away from wherever Bryant would expect me to be so he couldn't find me. Bringing my knees to my chest, I waited. I waited for whatever was to happen next, and I knew something would happen. I was now and had been under the impression I was being watched constantly. They found me when I was alone, and when I was with other people, they did not let it stop them. Insanity is objective; everyone has a motive for what they do whether or not it makes sense to others. Seagulls sang as they dove onto the sand and back up into the air again. They were my only company in a time of darkness. I left my phone at home, and since I have not had a watch since I was in seventh grade, time eluded me. My sister, smiling and alive, appeared in my head. Holidays were never perfect with our family, but we still had fun together. Every Christmas, we would wake up at four in the morning, tiptoeing down the stairs to see if Santa had arrived. The tree would be bright and beautiful, and sometimes the presents would be there, daring us to open them or they wouldn't. Our parents always left a window of opportunity so we wouldn't catch on. Our childhood wasn't perfect, but there were some highlights. Holidays were always one of them. Even with the fighting, there was something to think back on and smile about. I missed her more than anything; she deserved the world, but people don't always get what they deserve.

I felt something come across my face. I kicked up and flung myself onto my back. A figure was above me. I couldn't tell who it was, but a few guesses flashed across my mind before my vision went black and sleep found me.

CHAPTER 12

"You are full of surprises, I have to say I am very appreciative. You saved me time. I had a great plan to take you, really… You would have loved it." The room I woke up in was beautiful. It was white with a giant blue-and-green canopy and a gorgeous vanity. A giant door was off to the side, which I could only assume was a bathroom. My head was foggy, but I could still process my surroundings. Glancing down, I noticed I was on the canopy bed wearing a purple lace dress.

"What? Ben?" I blinked a few times as if it would wake me out of whatever dream I was in.

"Yes, my love?" In a second he was standing next to me and grabbed my hand.

"I'm not your love." I went to pull my other hand, but it jerked back. My right hand was cuffed to the bed.

He followed my gaze. "Oh sorry, I don't want you to be uncomfortable, but I realize we got off to a bad start before. Until you adjust to your new life, I thought it would be easier to keep you in one place for now." His smile landed on me, and he watched me intently as if in any moment I would confess my love for him in return.

"Where is Dakota?" I asked, shaking my head, trying to push the fog far out of my mind.

Ben's face turned dark. "He is no longer your concern. He can't bother you anymore."

I refused to accept that this might mean he was dead, but pushing the subject could only make him angrier. "Where am I?" This place was too nice for what Ben had been paid as an editor and even with Marcie's help…oh no. "Marcie…" I surveyed the room, almost expecting her to show up and make this nightmare worse.

"Oh, she won't bother us. By the way, she was just a means to an end. I plan on getting rid of her long before we get married." His eyes lit up at the thought.

"Married? You wanted to kill me." The fog disappeared, but the confusion settling in felt the same. He wanted to kill me; he had been trying to for months, but now he wanted to get married?

Nodding his head, enthusiastically, he said, "Absolutely! We got off to the wrong start, and we had some bumps on the road. Baby, I am so sorry for losing my temper. I did not handle jealousy well, but you know how I am. You know what you did was wrong, but I forgive you."

My mouth would have hung open if my mind could communicate with my body. I stared at him with an expression I could not describe, mostly because I couldn't see myself. His smile looked sweet, but his eyes looked crazed. He was without a doubt stuck in another world. What scared me the most was that I had never seen him like this. I remember when we met, back when he was normal. He was kind and innocent, but I always knew, in the back of mind, that something was way off. Ben moved over to the dresser directly across from the bed. He picked up what looked like an old ceramic teapot and poured the hot liquid into a smaller cup. He brought it over to me and lifted my head. "How are you feeling, my love?" I was sure the look on my face said it all. Watching him intently I could not decide how to respond. He tipped my head back and poured what I think might have been tea down my throat, but fear shook me. What if it was laced with something? As soon as he pulled it away, I spit it back out all over him. His smile evaporated, and fury covered his body. I could practically see the steam radiating off him. "That was really disrespectful, Arielle. After everything I have done for you, the least you could do is show me a little respect!" He took the teacup and hurled it at the wall; its shattered pieces carpeted the floor in seconds, along with the liquid. He huffed for a second, and then his hand was around my jaw and his face was inches away from mine. "You will learn your place with me, damn it! I need you to put in a little work for our relationship, all right?" His voice grew increasingly louder with every word. I stared at him, fueled by 90 percent rage and 10 percent terror. He was a deranged psychopath.

He stalked out of the room, slamming the door behind him. "Well, this is going to be fun." I rolled my eyes. Ben leaving gave me time to think and collect my thoughts. He did not plan on killing me now; he thought he could bring me to his side and love him. What made him change his mind? Quite frankly, dying would be less painful at this point, but this could give me the chance I need to escape. What was I going to do, though? I couldn't just convince him in a split second that after everything I would willingly be his wife; even in his deranged state he could not possibly believe that. I thought back to my case studies in college. I used some of them to create my characters, and if I focused hard enough, maybe I could fully understand his motives. Slowing down my breathing, I needed focus and patience. I've written this character; I could survive this. Glancing back up at my hand, I figured the first goal was to get him to trust me enough to remove the shackles. Even on a bed, my arm was extremely uncomfortable. There was a knock on the door, and it opened slowly. Red hair. "I was wondering when you were going to pay me a visit."

"A little snarky for someone cuffed to a bed, don't you think?" Marcie's grin was large enough to touch opposing walls.

"I'm done being your bitch. I am not a toy you can just play with." Maybe it was the faith that Ben was too in love with me at this point to kill me, or perhaps it was more of the fact that I felt like I had nothing left to lose. I could no longer show weakness.

Her laugh was more like a cackle, something you would expect from a fake witch in a low-budget documentary somewhere. "Oh, honey, you will never stop being my bitch…"

"How does it feel?" I lifted my head higher and forced my body to sit up right, arm still lifted over my head.

"What do you mean?" The smile had not left her face.

"To be a backup to me. He has me now, so he doesn't need you. He doesn't want you. Yet here you are, mocking me as if you won. I may be chained to this bed, but at least I'll be alive tomorrow. What about you? What does your future hold, Marcie?" I emphasized my words so they could sink in. I want one thing from her, and then I have nothing to worry about in terms of interference. I eyed the camera in the corner of the room; it was small and close to the ceiling, so it was possible she had no idea it was there. I knew he was watching; he had to be. I think it did the trick—she looked pained and angry. She stomped over, slapping me hard in the face, followed by her hands around my throat. At first her hands were light; her attempt was almost comical, but as the rage set in, her hands slowly clamped tighter around my throat. My airway was closing, and I was getting nervous. Kicking my legs in the air, trying to release from her grasp, did nothing.

Finally, after an eternity, the door bust open, and Ben ran in, grabbing Marcie by the arm and flinging her to the floor. "You do not get to put your hands on her! You are tainted!" he screamed at the top of his lungs. He smacked her across the face and pulled her by the arm, practically throwing her out of the room. He turned back to me briefly. I still choked on air, trying to get my breathing back on track. "She won't hurt you anymore, I promise." The door slowly closed. I heard harsh whispers and footsteps outside the door. Almost immediately, there was a large bang that echoed through the house. Did he shoot her? "Oh shit," I whispered. He had to have shot her. My ears were ringing, and everything was muffled. The door opened, and he was holding a gun. "Dinner will be ready around seven, I will come get you then," he said, and with that he closed the door.

I must have passed out waiting. Time was not being presented to me as it normally would have. My eyes slowly started to open, and for a split second, I expected to see the ocean. Bright and calming, seagulls were flying over my head looking for scraps of lunch from the children next door, and maybe even some music playing in the distance. Several weeks ago, I was lounging in my new house, and now I played the prisoner fiancée to my psychotic ex-editor. Amberley, Brennan, and Charmaine wouldn't die in vain. I'd been scared for far too long, but I could do this. I needed to channel my inner protagonist even if it would kill me. For a split second I almost forgot about Dakota. I needed to find him; he must be here, right? Hope rang in my mind, but I couldn't let that drive me, or can it? Ben opened the door with a smile on his face. "Hungry?" He unlocked the handcuffs and motioned for me to move off the bed. I did so slowly while rubbing my wrist, not fully expecting how uncomfortable and comfortable it would be to get released.

"Somewhat." He lifted my wrist to his mouth and kissed it while I tried not to vomit. "What's for dinner?" I walked into the hallway and noticed the blood was nowhere to be seen, but there was a medium-sized bottle of bleach outside the door.

"I ordered from an amazing Italian restaurant I think you'd love. They could cater our wedding reception if you'd like."

I nodded. "Sounds amazing, and uh...will Marcie be joining us?" He gave me a look that made me feel stupid for even trying to pretend we didn't both know that I knew what happened. I avoided his gaze. The house was small; the hallway wasn't large at least, and we passed three bedrooms including the one I was in before making it to the stairs. There was not a lot of furniture in the rooms, and the floors were definitely the original wood. It would have been a cute place if I wasn't being held captive. When we reached the stairs, I could tell from the inside the house had a very farmhouse-looking design. Were we still near the coast? I tried to get a peek outside, but Ben stepped into view.

"This way." He pointed to the dining room, which was set up to look fancier than it really was. It had a dining room table with a gorgeous tablecloth, which served as a host to two plates and sets of utensils with a glass at each end. "I know this place doesn't have much, but I just got it last week. The furniture should be arriving in a few days, and then we can make it a home." He pulled my chair out for me as I sat down slowly. What should I say that he would believe? He could call me on my bullshit sometimes, so I needed to be careful.

"It's a lovely house. When did you get it?" Before he sat down, he poured wine into our glasses. He had just opened the bottle, so I knew it was safe to drink and that I would definitely need to do. "Months ago, when you decided to move here temporarily. I figured I would get a place for us for when you were ready to take the next step. I knew it would be here. It's a magical place, isn't it? Perfect for starting a family."

Perfect for stabbing you in the throat. Okay, maybe not on the table, but it was tempting. My hands were not shackled, and I could potentially do it. I had to play the long game, right? I was not faster than him, and I had no idea where I really was. "It's so sweet of you to think of me like that. So we are close to my old place?" I took a sip of wine.

"Somewhat. I didn't want to be too far away from you especially with those two…losers following you around like puppies." The distaste on his face was evident; it was terrifying how delusional he clearly was. I tried not to react, especially when he turned to look at me to examine my reaction. He still didn't trust me, but he certainly wanted to, and I could work with that.

"You saved me. Thank you." Again, the vomit tried to come up as he nodded, clearly pleased with my acceptance of his intentions.

"I would do anything for you, Arielle. I honestly thought I would have to get rid of the rich one, but you did that all on your own. I knew you loved me." He started to eat, and I followed suit. I usually would be wary of the food, but I was starving. It seemed he would not hurt me for now as long as I played this game.

"That I do. So glad we can be together, wherever this place is." Come on, give me something! I needed to know where I was. "I have not been outside in a while. Maybe we could finish dinner outside?" I continued to eat and pretend like the request was nothing.

He started nodding. "You know"—he set his fork down and left his chicken and rice to sit—"I love that idea, but maybe tomorrow, okay? I just want to have a night in." He downed his drink. Chugging wine always seemed like a crime, but this was not the time to say anything.

"Okay, and I will probably need some things from my place… like my computer so I can work."

He laughed. "Baby, you will never have to work again!"

Fuck, that was not a good sign. When did Ben get so controlling? When did this behavior start? I watched him as if I was seeing him for the first time. On the outside, he looked to be in good spirits, but behind his dark eyes were pain, conflict, and confusion, so basically everything but happiness. I would feel pity in any other situation, but my awareness of his psychological state only pushed me further to escape. "So, what ever happened to Dakota?"

Ben's eyes went dark, and his sense of pleasantries went out the window in seconds. "He's close by, still breathing. If he's good, maybe we can let him go after the wedding. I just don't want him to ruin things." He was alive? Here I was prepared to plan another funeral.

"Thank you for not killing him" slipped out of my mouth when I meant to keep it in.

"You want him alive? Do you still have feelings for him?"

"No, not at all. I just am tired of bodies." I nudged my plate away and twirled my finger around the wine glass stem, avoiding his watchful eye. I wonder if Bryant had started looking for me. It'd been several hours at this point, so the cops must have been contacted. Maybe they could track my cell phone.

"I can admit"—he interrupted my thoughts—"it got out of hand, but I needed you to understand, and it worked. You came looking for me!" He gathered the plates and gestured for me to follow him. We passed the back door as we entered the kitchen. Sure enough, there were several padlocks and an alarm system bolted into the door. Perfect. So much for a trusting marriage. A laugh almost escaped me as I briefly forgot the insanity of the situation I was in.

"Can I ask you a question?" I had to know. I wonder if it was as easy as asking. A look of amusement crossed his face, as if I was some pet that was only here to entertain him, and with that the reality of my circumstances settled in. I was solely here for his amusement. I was not going to sit here and rack my brain trying to figure out what I did to deserve this. How was it that a crazy guy got the wrong idea about our connection, or lack thereof, and my first instinct was to blame myself? He nodded, urging me to continue. "When you came to visit my in my house, I heard another voice. Who was it?" He didn't blink, but his smile grew larger, and a small chuckle escaped his lips. It felt like an eternity had passed, but really it might have been three seconds. "You wouldn't believe me if I told you, so we will just leave it at that."

Ben brought me back to my room and didn't lock me to the bed; I considered this a plus. Was it too soon for him to trust me, or was this a test? I'd seen what he was capable of, so I couldn't take any chances. For importantly, there was someone else around here, but he had not presented himself. That kind of surprise was impossible to account for. Hours later he left me be, wanting me to get used to the room on my own and claimed he had some work to do, whatever that meant. I sure as hell knew he wasn't editing my novel, which wouldn't ever get finished at this point. I pushed that thought off; it was not an immediate concern anyway. The only window in the room was my saving grace. I tapped on it lightly; it was obviously made out of different material. There was no reverberation when I knocked on it, must have been bulletproof glass or whatever the super strong glass was called. It was getting dark outside, but that didn't change the view too much. The house was on a grassy hill, miles away from the main road, but it was still visible. Off to the side was the ocean, so we are still on the coast. The house was beautiful but needed work done, and he found it last minute. How did he find a house like this and in this kind of location? Pure luck? I didn't buy it for a second. Just when I thought it couldn't get any weirder, I knew some big puzzle pieces are missing.

After two weeks of watching his pattern, I learned a few things. He would come to see me in the morning around nine, and we would have breakfast. He would lead me down the stairs and would avoid the front door at all costs. I couldn't even say what it looked like. After the first week, Ben started bringing me to the back porch, and we would sit there while he forced me to write. He would take a look at what I was doing. Often times I did a good job, and other times he threw a tantrum and deleted thousands of words. Talk about working under pressure. He would always disappear between two and five, returning just before dinner, where we would eat together by the back patio. No one came over; there was no sign of life or existence outside of this house. After dinner, he would talk about the wedding; he could not decide if he wanted to elope or invite everyone. Surely, somewhere deep down he knew eloping was the only option. If anyone found us together, they would arrest him on the spot. He might be insane, but there was a method to his madness. Otherwise he would not have been getting away with it. Regardless, I found my opening. Three hours a day I was left unattended in this house. I just needed to figure out a way to get past the locked doors.

I was never a badass in school. I hung out with a small group of innocent kids, so it was safe to say I had no idea how to pick a lock. I was confident if I broke it, I would only have one shot of getting out before he figured out my plan. The window certainly wasn't an option…or was it? I walked over to the window. How do you break an unbreakable window? No, not possible! The only option was to break the door, but even so, it was extremely risky, and I couldn't say for sure it would be worth it at this point. Then again, how long could I keep this going? Another few weeks, months, years? No way in hell, that was not happening.

One day Ben came barging in all out of sorts. "They won't let it go! They don't understand, you are mine! Mine!" I watched him with wide eyes. He looked like the Hulk but a lot smaller and less green.

"Who?" I asked quietly. When he was angry, he got violent, and I'd rather not stand in his path. Sitting on the bed playing my part, I hoped he meant someone who was close to getting me out of here, but I knew I was not having much luck.

"Those stupid cops, stupid, stupid cops!" He paced back and forth, banging his fists against his head. Maybe if I'm lucky, he would accidentally knock himself out. Over the last few weeks, I had tried to not let the panic or stress get to me. Staying positive was near impossible when there was no end in sight. I prayed those stupid, stupid cops would figure out what happened, but considering they couldn't even locate him once over the last several months, there was no way they would find him or me now. I heard a small creak in the background as he continued to pace. Words were spewing from his mouth, but I couldn't hear what they were. I was too focused on the door he left cracked open, unlocked, right in front of me. "They know nothing! They think I am some crazy person! Well, I am not crazy!" he continued to shout. Practically leaping toward the dresser, he flung his arms and knocked over all the things he had left there for me: jewelry boxes, figurines of dogs, random knickknacks. They all fell to the ground; some of them breaking and others simply rolling around the floor. I could feel my face shift to amusement, but I couldn't express that. I was trying not to focus on the door too much while planning my next steps. "Okay, that might have been a little crazy, but aside from that, I am not insane!" He walked over to the wall and started banging his head on it. Yeah, totally sane. I couldn't believe this; I had one shot. He continued to bang his head against the wall, loudly screaming, and my feet were the first to know what needed to happen. I tiptoed to the door slowly, opened it, it creaked loudly. Then I was running.

My heart started to beat so fast I thought I might pass out. Nausea hit me hard out of anxiety. I eventually heard the head banging stop. "Arielle? What are you doing!" Suddenly, I heard larger footsteps as I bounded down the hall and got to the stairs. Landing on the last step, I saw the front door was in sight. I had to hit it and keep running. Two steps at a time and in a moment, I was knocked on my ass. I hit something; did I run into the door? Everything was spinning. No, I hit a body. It had to be a body. I looked up. "Bryant? Oh my god, it's you!" A smile spread across my face; he was here to save me. He found me! I could kiss that man.

Ben reached the landing and slowed. Bryant was going to kick his ass. Bryant watched me and helped me up. "Hey, beautiful." He kissed me. I could feel Ben's eyes on us, but I didn't care. I was finally safe.

"You found me."

"Found you? I never lost you." His eyes looked different. Something in the way he looked at me was wrong.

"What? What do you mean…" I backed up, but his grip on my shoulders tightened.

"How did she get away from you? How much of a moron could you be? She is three times smaller than you." His eyes darted to Ben.

"Give me a break. She caught me in a moment, and let go of her. She isn't yours anymore."

"We had an agreement. You fulfilled your end. Where is that crazy bitch that keeps following you around?" My world was spinning, almost literally it felt like. Bryant was the mystery guy? He was the one helping Ben and Marcie this entire time? Ben and Bryant exchanged words, but only a few registered. He had been with me for months, standing by my side and protecting me. It all made sense now; I should have trusted my gut. Now what? My breathing picked up speed; I was going to pass out. My body got hot, and sweat began to drip down my forehead.

"Oh, Arielle, you probably have so many questions." Bryant had the same look in his eye as Ben. The Bryant I knew was gone, or maybe he just never existed.

"You said I would get to keep her. She belongs to me!" Ben was whining in the background; it was sickening, but I was getting used to it.

"Will you shut the fuck up? You are the biggest baby I have ever met." Ben's anger got the best of him as he lunged for Bryant. Without fault or hesitation, Bryant grabbed Ben by the neck and twisted it in a split second. Ben's head snapped, and he went down hard. My mouth dropped as I watched his body hit the floor, and just like that stalker number one was done for. My eyes slowly drifted to Bryant, who stood there staring at Ben's oversized body and shrugged as if taking a life meant nothing.

"You…" The words could not come out; there were none to express. I couldn't say I loved him. I never did, but I could have. My friend, my lover, my stalker—and I could no longer see him for who he was but who he is.

"Yes, me. Look, Ari…don't take offense. I did it for the same reason Ben did. I love you. Your creativity is inspiring." He stroked my face slowly. "But you have to understand, or maybe you don't, you have been tainted by fame, by the world." His kind eyes watched me. What he was looking for I couldn't say, my brain was shutting down. "I want to cleanse you of this sin. Would you like to be cleansed, Ari?"

Frozen. The words he spoke were registering, but my brain didn't want to accept this was my new reality. Anyone but him. He grabbed my face with both hands and jerked it forward. "I asked you a question." His tone was even, but his eyes were malicious and dark.

"Go to hell," I mumbled through his grasp.

"All right then, closet time."

CHAPTER 13

Darkness, it surrounded me and pulled me close. He pushed me into a small room big enough for two people. But it was just for me. He slammed the door shut and locked the door. I felt nothing near me; it was bare. He took my clothes and only left me in my underwear. Feeling exposed and scared, I tried taking deep breaths. This was too much. He was there for me when no one else was, and he was the one ruining my life. I should have listened to my gut, but instead I desperately sought for solace in the one person I shouldn't have. Dakota was probably dead, like everyone else. Unless he was in on it too? Screw this. If I made it out of here alive, I was moving back home. "Arielle, can you hear me?" His voice echoed in the room. Looking around, I saw no window or person with me. "I installed speakers so we can do this together. You need to be purified, Arielle, and that starts now!"

Cold water hit me quickly, falling down on me like a shower. "Holy shit!" I screamed and clutched my arms tight, trying to shield myself from the freezing cold water hitting every inch of my body.

"To be cleansed is a privilege, Arielle. You have been chosen by me!" I wanted to knock those speakers off whatever they were hooked to. I gritted my teeth and hovered in one of the corners. My hair was drenched, and with every cold drop, the bumps on my arm got worse. Seconds passed, minutes passed. How long was this going to go on? At what point would Bryant the Devil believe I was cleansed?

"Make it stop! I'll do whatever you want, just make it stop!" I screamed after what felt like an eternity. Nothing...he chose this moment to be silent. I was too frozen to cry, but I felt it bubbling in me. I focused my mind. I had to, or I'd go insane. I couldn't let this monster break me. I didn't think anyone could be worse than Ben. Turned out that little bitch had a puppet master. Amberley, Charmaine, Brennan...I needed to do this for them. Dakota, he didn't deserve this. He was the good one, and I took advantage of him. Not purposely, but I did. Kira—who knows what Bryant had done to her. There was so much good that came out of moving here, but just as much, if not more bad, had stemmed from it as well. If I could go back, I would. I would have stayed where I was and never headed east. This town was a curse. Remembering all I had lost made me want to cry more. How could I focus on anything positive right now? He said he was trying to purify me, but I think he was trying to break me. Jokes on him, I was already broken. I remained silent; begging did nothing, but I could at least pretend I was strong. Think of the novel, think of the success, you did that! Another voice inside my head told me that those successes got me here, trapped in a half water hole, half dark closet torture room. The speakers began to sound again. It was my voice and then his. What the hell? He was playing our phone conversations, our dates. He recorded all of them! They went painfully slow; I remembered every single one from our first date to telling him about Kira to the last night I saw him. He sounded so genuine, so real, but it was all fake. It was a show.

After a while, the sound and water stopped at the same time. I stood there in disbelief. Was it over? "Round two," he emitted from the speaker box.

"Round two?" It started to warm up. It felt nice at first after the freezing cold shower I was forced into for who knew how long.

"You handled an hour of that. Let's see what happens with two hours of this? Will you be cleansed by heat, Arielle?" Heat? What kind of sick, twisted room was this? The room progressively got warmer until it felt like I would pass out. Sweat dripped down my forehead and down my entire body. I felt like someone hosed me down while I stood on the sun. The speaker started again, but this time with screams and crying. "No! God, please, don't, please!" It was Charmaine's voice. Brennan's scream was in the background; loud noises and something shattering distracted me. He recorded their deaths. He killed them, not Ben. "I made this for you so you could understand what you caused. You did this, not me."

Rage surged through me, but the energy itself could not be displayed. I felt weaker and weaker by the moment, wishing the cold water would come back. That was unpleasant, but this could actually kill me. Feeling the heat wrap around me, I could swear my skin was bubbling, but as I felt my arms, it was smooth and dry. Various screams and whimpers echoed in my death box. I felt them in my body, and my heart broke all over again. I knew they paid the cost, but to hear it and feel it was another thing entirely. I was not sure how long I was up before I dropped to my knees; the air was diminishing. I was going to die in here, being purified by a maniac. I no longer felt the heat as my eyes shut. I woke back up to screams, but the heat was gone. Covered in sweat and unable to stand, I knocked on the door lightly in desperation. I couldn't take anymore, I couldn't do this. Just kill me already! The door opened, and I dropped to the side, half of my body hanging outside of the room. I felt Bryant drag me out of the room. My eyes would open and shut. I felt him lift me up and lay me on something flat and cold. My eyes fluttered, trying to stay open, but all I could see was a fridge and a sink. I must be in the kitchen. I was out just as quickly as I was awake. Noises in the background urged me to stay awake, but my body was too weak and my mind was not far behind. "Stop." Was that my voice? It didn't sound like me at all.

"You are not done being purified, Arielle, but don't worry, you will be soon." I saw a giant knife being held over me.

When I was younger, I never thought much about the future. Where I would go to school, what job I wanted, marriage, and I especially never thought about how I would die. I usually spent my time listening to music and thinking about the next day, and that was as far as I ever got into planning my life. At one point in high school, I figured I enjoyed writing and creating, always having this romanticized notion of being a writer on the East Coast, and when I moved here, I was thrilled. I never expected to be the subject of someone's obsession, let alone be on a table while some hot psychopath carved into me. The first twinge of pain was enough for me to pass out.

I've never woken up on a table before. The sunlight streamed in through the little windows that lined the counters, and I felt safe for a split second. My chest had blood on it. I patted myself down to check to make sure that all my body parts were attached, which was a bonus. My chest was sticky, and my shirt clung to it. A stinging sensation made me shiver. Bryant was nowhere to be seen. I unbuttoned my blouse a bit more to see clumps of blood and droplets all over my chest. He carved into me a word or something. It hurt like a bitch. I needed to get showered.

Bryant walked in with a cup of coffee in his hand. "Aw, you're awake. How do you feel?"

I stared down at my chest. *Pure*—that was what it said! I glanced up at him, trying to hide my awe, and the exhaustion helped me. "I feel…pure?" I responded, hoping it would make things easier.

His smile, for a split second, reminded me of the Bryant I once knew. "Success! Oh, I am so glad to hear that." He set his cup of coffee down. "How about you take a nice shower and join me for breakfast?"

What was it with these guys and sitting down for meals? I don't want to spend time with you! "I am very tired. Sleeping on the table didn't help my back. Would you mind if I took a shower and went to bed?"

His eyes darkened but lightened up. "I think that is a great idea. Also, tomorrow we will be heading back to my house. This place is a shithole, and you'd deserve better." He guided me to the stairs and watched me walk up every single one. I tried not to eye the door as I did. "Oh, Arielle?"

"Yes?" I grabbed the banister tightly.

"Don't try anything stupid. I'm not Ben." And with that he walked into another room, which I assume was the living room minus the living part. I stood there, watching my only escape route being monitored by my ex-lover and friend. You couldn't write this crap. Maybe I would if I could escape this mess. Every single day took a piece of my hope away, but there was still a small part of me that wanted to fight, if I only had the energy.

The freedom I was allowed to have while showering and getting dressed was unusual. I was a prisoner here, but I was also free as long as I played by the rules. I pulled a random blue T-shirt out of a drawer that Ben or Bryant grabbed for me at the store. As I shimmied it on, I watched the front of the house from the window. I could run; I just don't know which way to go. I saw a small town in the distance, but he might have a car to chase me down or a gun to shoot me from afar. Both options sounded terrifying, but I could try. I just needed an opening. Dakota flashed in my mind. Where was he? If he was here, I couldn't just leave him, because Bryant would for sure kill him. No, I have to stay here until I find him. The house wasn't large, but even Bryant said we were leaving soon to his ridiculously large house. Could he be here or at the other place? Was there a basement? Was he getting tortured?

There was a knock on the door. "What's taking so long?"

I pulled on a pair of jeans and opened the door. "I was just getting dressed." Closing the door behind me, we went downstairs. When he grabbed my hand, it took everything in me to not pull away. As we neared the bottom step, I heard a clanking. My ears could be ringing from the closet of doom, but I could swear something was making noise. There was a small vent near the bottom of the stairs. More clanking—it must be coming from the basement. Keeping my suspicions at bay, Bryant watched me as we rounded the corner, and he guided me to the porch. I had to find a way down to that basement.

"Look around, Arielle, do you see anyone or anything?" Bryant pointed out to the front of the house. Aside from a long winding road and a lot of trees, I saw nothing from this vantage point, but I knew there was a town close by. I shook my head. He grabbed my shoulders softly. "I know you want nothing to do with me now. I also know you are strong-willed, so for the sake of your safety, I am going to tell you this, and I am only going to say it once. Outside of the house there is a fifty-foot perimeter. If you try to pass that perimeter, you will get shocked at a hundred milliamps which will cause ventricular fibrillation of the heart. You will die." I watched the area in shock. He thought of everything. There goes my plan of running! He smiled at me. "So I know the temptation is there, but don't do it. I will still be leaving this place today to wrap up some things before we head back to the house. We should only be there a day or two before we fly to London. I have some business to attend there." With that, he turned and walked back into the house. How could I get shocked but he could walk out without an issue? He grabbed a small bag from beside the door and headed to an old silver sports car. What brand, I couldn't say. "I will see you in a few hours. Behave!" I watched as he drove away. Looking down at my chest, I realized he did not just carve a word into my body, he planted something in there. Once the truck was out of sight, I ran into the house and into the bathroom. On my way up, I noticed there were no cameras, which was surprising considering everything else he thought of to keep me here. I guess overconfidence got the best of him—if only I could find a way to use that to my advantage. Standing in front of the mirror, taking the T-shirt off, I flinched as I saw the word *pure* carved into my body. I felt around the lettering for an extra sore or hard spot. Above my left collar bone…ouch! I saw it, a quarter-sized purple bruise above the *e*. How could something that small send that many volts to my body? I guess it didn't help that it was right near my heart. I was not a doctor; how was I going to get this out? I touched it; holy shit, that was unpleasant. What if I jabbed it with a knife and it would go off? No, the only way it would was if I crossed the barrier with it. I had three hours to figure this out! Wait, the basement! Running down the stairs, trying to hit every turn without sliding across the wooden floor, I tore down the hallway looking for a door that didn't lead to the death box. Around the corner from it though was a similar-looking door with a padlock on it. I really need to learn how to pick a lock. Good grief.

There had to be a toolbox around here somewhere. The next fifteen minutes was spent looking for a large heavy object that I could lift to break the padlock. I tried a vacuum, which was more difficult than I expected it to be until I found a hammer in one of the drawers in the kitchen. Luckily, even psychos have a junk drawer with a random list of stuff. Every swing and hit that I was able to get shook my body to its core; it didn't help that my chest was extremely sore from being carved like a pumpkin. After what felt like an eternity, the padlock broke. I was beginning to think I was going to fail at this. There was a stairway with no light switch. On each stair was a small blue LED strip. Interesting choice, but okay. Slowly I took each step, careful not to set off another potential trap that ridiculous man might have set. Then again, there was no way he would give me enough credit to successfully break that padlock. As I reached the bottom, I saw the basement was empty except for a large dog cage in the corner. There was a figure on the floor in gray sweatpants and nothing else. "Dakota?" I whispered.

The body slowly turned over, and Dakota's beautiful eyes stared back at me but with less life than usual. He was beaten and bloodied; his eyes widened at the sight of me. "Are you real?" His voice was hoarse. I nodded, and he stood up slowly but fell into the bars. "Agh!" He clutched his side.

I ran to him, looking for a way out. "Okay, hold on one second!" I ran back upstairs and grabbed the hammer. I jumped several steps, making my way back to him. "Bryant...Bryant is the killer," he said.

I laughed. "Yeah, I learned that."

"You have the worst taste in guys." I broke the lock, and he leaned into me. I kissed him like I haven't seen him in months.

"Not all guys, but look, he will be gone for another two hours. We need to get out of here now!"

He draped his arm around my shoulder. "I will try to move as fast as I can. I think my ribcage is broken." We hobbled up the stairs. It must have been a sight to be seen; I was carrying the weight of a grown man as he leaned on someone a good foot shorter than him. Before making it to the porch, I said, "Wait,

wait!" I stopped, turned him into the living room, and plopped him on the chair.

"What? You said we needed to go!" He pointed to the door frantically.

"We do, but before we do, I need you to cut my chest open."

"Sorry, you want me to do what?" I had never seen Dakota look as panicked as he did now, even in the basement locked up like a wild animal. I rolled my eyes. Right, he missed the evil monologue.

"Bryant set up a perimeter with some kind of signal register." I unbuttoned my shirt and pointed to the purple bruise. "He carved this into me and installed some kind of chip. If I try to cross that perimeter with this chip in me, I will get electrocuted, and it will stop my heart."

Dakota's mouth was wide open. "Fuck."

"Yeah, my thoughts exactly. So I need you to get it out and quickly. We have to travel by foot, and you are in no shape to run." He started nodding in disbelief, but I knew he was up to it. I mean…he was a part time fisherman.

Fumbling through a few drawers in the kitchen and bathroom, I found a small incision knife and a few bandages, I also grabbed a bottle of whiskey from the pantry. Pouring the whiskey on the knife, I handed it to Dakota, and I rolled my T-shirt up and stuffed it in my mouth. He slowly cut through the bruise. Blood trickled out as he pushed deeper around the wound, trying to fish out the chip. "Mhmmgrhhh."

"I know, I know." He put one hand on my right shoulder so I wouldn't step back. "Almost there."

I wanted to pass out, but this was the least amount of pain I had been in for weeks. More blood trickled out. "Mmmmurry." I clenched the shirt with my teeth. He pulled the chip out, and I fell back, spitting the shirt out of my mouth. "That was hell." I tried catching my breath. Dabbing the blood and pouring some alcohol on it burned even more. I settled the bandage on it and helped Dakota up. "Okay, we need to get as close to town as possible. It was maybe two or three miles down the road!" Dakota rolled his eyes as if that were an easy feat in our conditions.

Three months ago, I never could imagine that those horror stories I saw on the news could be me. Sheltered and hidden from the horrors of real life was worse than I could have ever dreamed of in any book I could ever write or any film that could ever be made. Dakota moved hunched forward and limping, while I flinched every other second from pressure being put on my chest. I was not the same woman I was when I got here. I was lazy and naive. I had plans, but what meaning did they have? What purpose did my life serve aside from entertaining others and making money? We crossed the grounds. The road was so close, and someone was walking in our direction.

"Hey! Hey!" I started waving at the stranger and yelling.

The stranger turned toward us, stopped, and started running. They pulled out a phone as they reached us. "Are you okay?" The man was about Dakota's height but plushy. He scratched his beard as we heard, "Nine-one-one, what's your emergency?"

"I found her, I found Arielle Taylor and that Lawrence man…" He gave the dispatcher the address and hung up the phone. The man went to lift Dakota off me so he could get him closer to the road just as a truck turned into the driveway. The truck stopped, and Bryant stepped out with a gun. He started shooting quickly. The three of us dropped to the ground. The man who was helping us was grunting, and as I turned to look at him, blood was flooding from his chest. Dakota tried to crawl on top of me to shield me from any other bullets heading our way. "I told you you would die if you crossed that barrier without me, Arielle. You should have listened! We could have been great together!" Another shot—where it went, I had no idea, but Dakota was still breathing. Police sirens went off; they were closing in but still far enough away that if Bryant tried to shoot us again, he could very well hit us this time.

Several cops' cars pulled into the lot. "Put the gun down! Put the gun down!" several of the officers yelled. Dakota and I slowly got up, but Bryant did not take his eyes off us.

"You and I could have been together. I almost forgave you for your indiscretions, but you refused to stop seeing him!" He sneered at Dakota.

"Burn in hell, you rich prick."

Bryant lifted the gun once more. Dakota moved in front of me the same time one of the officers shot their gun directly at Bryant. He went down quickly and didn't move. Was he dead? Part of me wanted him dead, but the other half of me wanted him alive so he could rot in prison. My heart skipped a beat; the anticipation was going to kill me, not these wounds. The cops moved in on him as did an ambulance. He was moved, so he must have still been alive. Two cops came over to us and led us to the second ambulance. "We have been looking everywhere for you," the sheriff said with a smile.

"No offense, but you really need better training." Dakota laughed as they laid him back on the gurney.

Bryant was put into one as well. "He is going away for a long time, if he even survives that shot." The sheriff turned and walked away, tipping his hat as he did. The cops swarmed the house and took my statement as Dakota headed to the hospital, this time in a legitimate ambulance. As he left, a news crew showed up and spread out all over the place, getting shots of the house and asking me questions. Two cops escorted me to their car and offered me a ride to the hospital to get my battle scars checked for infection. Watching the house get farther and farther behind us as we drove away was liberating. Tears flowed almost immediately as I realized I actually won. Somehow, despite everything, I get to live without fear anymore.

Two months later

I never moved back home, but I definitely didn't stay in Rhode Island. Dakota's ribcage was almost healed, and I was sewn up all nice and proper, but the word *pure* still laid across my chest. It was a reminder I would never get rid of. According to the doctors, it might fade sure, but it would never truly be gone. I was okay with that. It reminded me of the strength and fight that I had in me every step of the way. Even when I felt I was crumbling apart, I pushed forward. My mother started sending me pictures of Amberley's grave site, and when I was ready, I would one day go to visit Charmaine and Brennan, but it was still too soon. Before leaving Rhode Island, we found Kira. Well, actually, the cops did when they investigated Bryant's house. Although he was crazy, he was legitimately taking care of Kira, and that I was thankful for, more so that she was alive because it was hard to feel grateful toward him for anything.

The cops found Ben and Marcie's bodies on the premises. Bryant was sentenced to life in prison with no chance of parole on six counts of murder. Unfortunately, the kind man who saved us did not make it, but we were forever grateful. His name was Leonard Basins; he had two children and one grandchild. Dakota sold his store before he was ever discharged from the hospital. We packed up the stuff we wanted and moved to Massachusetts, some small town twenty minutes from Salem. I ended up taking a concealed carry class as soon as I passed a psych eval due to the torture he put me through. I was never going to feel helpless ever again, and I easily persuaded Dakota to do the same. We would go to the gun range once a week now.

Dakota sat with me on the couch, cuddled up in front of the TV. The wind flowed through the open house. The only way I could describe this kind of peace was pure bliss. Kira chased her tail and plopped on the ground. My publishers sent flowers and gift baskets constantly. I was able to finish my final installment, and along with the publicity of my kidnapping, book sales skyrocketed. After settling into our new home, both Dakota and I did a few interviews. I had volunteered my time to spreading awareness of stranger danger, as silly as that sounded. I quickly learned there was nothing silly about staying alive. "Arielle?"

I looked up at him, wanting to smile, wanting to tell him that I love him, but I can't. I knew he had been wanting to, but neither one of us wanted to feel it was forced due to the trauma we experienced. I feel strongly for him and maybe at one time, I would have accepted the feeling of love.

Dakota switched the movie off and turned on the news. We tried to keep up on it more for awareness sake. If someone were to go missing like we did, then we wanted to make sure we knew everything about it so we could help out, just like Leonard Basins did for us. He continued to kiss me, the world seemed a lot less evil. I never considered myself a sappy and emotional woman, but this man stuck with me during the hardest times, and after everything, there was no way I was not going to embrace the possibility of love. "Breaking news—it was just learned that two days ago, murderer of six and multimillionaire business entrepreneur Bryant Feld escaped from prison. Mr. Feld was charged with life without parole after he stalked and nearly killed famous writer Arielle Taylor and her friend Dakota Lawrence. His victims were plenty, and he was caught just two months ago by local Rhode Island police…"

Dakota and I stared at the TV. Anxiety hit me like a brick. I leaned forward; vomit hit the coffee table as Kira stood up and started barking. Dakota went over to her. "Shhh, Kira, it's okay." He watched me. "Babe, don't worry, they will catch him before he even finds out where we are." The look on his face did not match the confidence he tried to convey with his words.

"This cannot happen again. Why, why is this devil so hard to keep in one place? He's a fucking businessman, not a ninja!" I tried to slow my breathing, one in and one out.

There was a knock on the door.

ABOUT THE AUTHOR

KAYLA SERRANO HAS BEEN DEVELOPING HER CRAFT FROM A YOUNG AGE AND DOVE further into her interests in the thriller and supernatural genres. She holds a bachelor's degree in communications from Ohio Dominican University and a master's degree in creative writing from Tiffin University. Kayla lives in Columbus, Ohio, with her family and lovable canines.

CPSIA information can be obtained
at www.ICGtesting.com
Printed in the USA
BVHW031424280621
610633BV00002B/456